# The Long-Cursed Map

# Brass and Glass, Book 2

Dawn Vogel

Cover Art by J. Kathleen Cheney

2nd Edition
Originally published by Razorgirl Press
Copyright 2018 Dawn Vogel
All rights reserved.
ISBN: 1-948280-18-3     ISBN: 13 978-1-948280-18-1

# DEDICATION

To everyone who asked, "Is the robot going to be okay?"
Welcome back.

**Books in the Brass & Glass Series**
*The Cask of Cranglimmering*
*The Long-Cursed Map*
*The Boiling Sea*

# CONTENTS

# CHAPTER ONE

Svetlana and Athos had been in hot water before, but never quite like this. The captain and first mate of *The Silent Monsoon* excelled at both getting themselves into sticky situations and finding their way out, but this time, Captain Svetlana Tereshchenko didn't see any potential exits.

*The Flaming Pony*'s crew members were scavengers, an assortment of brutish ruffians and nimble thieves who worked together to keep a steady flow of not-entirely-legal merchandise moving between platform cities, suspended above the boiling ocean through a combination of geysers and engines. They seemed to have sent the most menacing of the bunch to stop Svetlana and her crew.

"Listen," Athos said, a broad smile plastered across his face and twinkling in his eyes. "We're happy to pay for the parts we need."

Svetlana stomped on the side of Athos's boot. They had known each other for a decade and a half, so they often didn't need words to communicate. In this case, they both knew they couldn't afford the parts Indigo needed.

Sneaking on to *The Flaming Pony* had been simple, even with the lanky, awkward mechanic, Indigo, in tow. But his rummaging around in their scrap room had caused an avalanche of spare parts. The crash had drawn the crew's attention, which now put Svetlana and Athos between that crew and a locked pine door.

"Right. We'd be happy to negotiate some sort of trade or payment plan?" Athos suggested.

One of the men, deeply tanned, shirtless, and muscular, shook his head, causing his wispy mustache, which was the sum total of all the hair visible on his body, to swish back and forth. Gesturing toward the scrap room with a jagged knife, he growled, "How's

1

about you put everything back where you found it, and tell that blue-haired freak—"

Svetlana didn't let the aeronaut finish. She slashed at his bare arm with her boot knife. "How about no?" she snarled.

Her blade connected. The aeronaut bellowed in pain before he lunged toward Svetlana. His knife blade went far astray of his mark. The other members of the crew behind him surged forward, but the hallway was too narrow for any but the smallest of them to get past.

"Indy! Hurry up! We're leaving now," Svetlana called out.

"Need more stuff," Indigo called from inside the scrap room.

Two smaller crew members, scruffily dressed with shaggy hair, swaggered toward Svetlana with sharpened sticks, but neither of them had as much reach with their weapons as she did with her knife. While the larger crew member in front focused on covering the wound she had given him, Svetlana kicked at one of the smaller crew members, landing her blow on their wrist. They yelped in pain and dropped their stick, while their compatriot slipped back into the crowd, not wanting to see what Svetlana would do next.

"We'll have to find another source," Svetlana called toward the scrap room. "The customer service here is awful."

*The Flaming Pony* was a flying junkyard, the place where unwanted parts went to be forgotten. Like Svetlana's own airship, it was a repurposed sailing ship, fitted out with steam-filled balloons that helped with elevation, propelled by a steam-powered engine. It was an efficient system, albeit overly dependent on a steady supply of coal to keep gallons of water in gaseous form.

Svetlana told herself that stealing from thieves was better than stealing from honest businessmen, but the truth of the matter was that this ship was an easier target than many others. That was the whole reason they were on *The Flaming Pony* in the first place. Svetlana and her crew needed to obtain supplies to repair Drassilis, the deactivated automaton they had hauled with them when they left Bonebriar. They had high hopes that he would have information about a map that they'd been pursuing.

"You got a plan for getting us out, Cap?" Athos asked, his voice quivering only slightly, but his eyes betraying his realization that they might have gotten themselves into more trouble than they'd planned for.

The narrow hallway ahead of them was packed tight with a throng of menacing men and women. To their immediate left was the entrance to the scrap room, which Svetlana and Athos had been defending so that none of the crew could reach Indigo. Hazarding a backward glance, Svetlana checked that the door behind them opened away from the mob. There should be a way out if they retreated. At least, there would be if they were on *The Silent Monsoon*. That no one had come through the door to block their departure was worrisome, and they'd need to haul Indigo out to take him with them.

"That's a door behind us, isn't it?" Svetlana said, trying to ease Athos's nerves with a joke. "Hold them off for a minute and let me see if I can get it open."

"Oh, sure, you take the easy route," Athos scoffed.

"Hardly," Svetlana said. "Step two involves extracting Indy."

Athos shoved his unruly brown and blond curls out of his eyes with one hand, raised his knife, and let Svetlana switch places with him. "Fair," he said, trading blows with the crew member whose arm Svetlana had slashed, still the only one who remained in a position where he could fight with them.

Once Svetlana fully assessed the door, she was certain they could use it as their means of escape. There was enough space between the door and the jamb that Svetlana could easily slip her knife blade in and release the catch. She only gave a moment's thought to the fact that the door could only have been secured from the other side.

"The door's unlocked," she murmured as she passed Athos on her way into the scrap room.

"Why didn't you say that before?" he asked, a note of exasperation creeping into his voice.

Svetlana shrugged. "Because it wasn't then."

Metal on metal clanged outside, as Athos continued to hold off the crew members, but the din in the scrap room was cacophonous. Indigo had festooned himself with wires, tubes, and some sort of metal mesh, while his arms and rucksack were filled with parts that he couldn't wear. He even balanced a flat piece of metal with a few more parts stacked atop it on his head, in the middle of a blue halo of hair flared out from some unseen source of static electricity.

"Indy, what else do you need?"

"Six more arms?" he suggested, using one foot to poke at a pile.

"We've only got four more, at best, and we're probably going to need a couple of those for fighting." Spying another bag in one of the piles, Svetlana snatched it and held it out for Indigo to dump some of what he was holding.

"Cap, you said a minute," Athos called from the hallway.

"On our way!" she replied, slinging the bag over her shoulder.

"I *need* more parts," Indigo insisted, his teenaged voice suddenly higher-pitched than it had been a moment earlier.

"We'll have to get the rest somewhere else." Grabbing Indigo by the collar, Svetlana dragged the boy into the hallway.

The situation there had not improved, but Svetlana's planned escape route was still open. She moved ahead of Indigo and pulled him along the hallway. "Time to retreat," she said, pushing the door open.

"About time," Athos said with a heavy sigh. "Sorry, gents. Not enough of me to go around, and you don't seem like the sharing type." A slamming sound, followed by splintering wood, heralded Athos's arrival in the retreat. "That won't keep them long. Do you know where you're going?"

"Not a clue," Svetlana said. "But this hallway has to lead somewhere."

It was only when she realized how much warmer she was in front that she understood how this ship was laid out. They'd escaped their attackers only to dead end at the ...

"Boiler room," Indigo said.

Svetlana cursed under her breath. A young man with swirling blue-black tattoos covering his deep sepia brown forearms and hands, whom Svetlana assumed must be the ship's mechanic, was fast asleep in his hammock, even with her, Athos, and Indigo standing over him. Though he wasn't trying to stop them yet, the rest of the crew members would be breathing down their necks at any moment.

"Up," Indigo said, gesturing at the ceiling of the boiler room.

Scanning the ceiling, Svetlana shook her head. "That's all well and good on the *Monsoon*, but it doesn't look like they've got a hatch here."

"We could make one," Athos said, drawing his pistol.

"I hardly think that's the best plan," Svetlana said.

"You got a better one?"

4

Svetlana looked around the boiler room. The mechanic was just now waking up, but he looked groggy enough that she didn't think he would be a threat. There were portholes that Indigo could squeeze through, but since *The Flaming Pony* was in flight, that wasn't a good option. "We need a distraction."

Indigo nodded and began tinkering with the boiler. A loud whine followed, and steam began billowing from one of the valves, clouding the boiler room.

"Don't get too close," Indigo said from somewhere within the cloud. "It's hot."

Svetlana nodded, her brow creased. "How do we get out? Down?"

The muffled shouts of the crew members who had been pursuing Svetlana and her crew were audible over the hissing of the boiler. Svetlana turned to find the mechanic and pointed her knife at him. "You got a name?"

He glanced at Svetlana, Athos, and Indigo in turn, as though he were assessing the odds of one of them stabbing him. He raised his hands slowly. "Buck."

"Nice to meet you, Buck. How do we get out of here without going the way we came?"

"Down's the chiller for recycling the water; don't want to shoot the floor in here."

"Up, then?"

"I'm gonna grab that broom handle—" Buck put his hands up and pointed at a stick near his hammock. "—and open the hatch for ya. Alright?"

Svetlana nodded, still keeping her knife trained in Buck's direction.

Buck used the broom handle to move aside a previously unseen ceiling panel. "No ladder, but you can use the hammock for a boost." He shook his head. "Then you're on your own."

"Better than nothing." Svetlana tucked away her knife, climbed into the hammock, and looked through the hole in the ceiling. The blue sky beyond made her grin. She grabbed the sides of the hole and pulled herself through.

Reaching a hand down to help Indigo through, she smiled at Buck. "It's nothing personal, really. You just have the stuff we need."

5

"Understood," Buck said. "Part and parcel of the business. But if we see you again, we're not gonna be so nice."

"Fair," Svetlana said. With Indigo hoisted up on deck, she held up a finger to Athos. She had a couple of Quinpence in her purse, and she tossed them down to Buck with a shrug. "It's something, at least."

"That it is," he replied.

Athos hauled himself through the hole, his ropy muscles bulging as he did. He glanced at Svetlana. "He's just gonna let us go for a couple of Quinpence?"

"No, I anticipate something'll come around before we make it out of here," Svetlana said.

"Ship's too far," Indigo called out from the edge of the deck.

Svetlana and Athos joined him. *The Silent Monsoon* was pacing *The Flaming Pony*, but Jo was keeping her distance. Svetlana waved her red handkerchief in that direction. For a long moment, nothing happened, but then her ship slowed slightly, preparing to move alongside *The Flaming Pony*.

"Yep, here comes trouble," Athos said, glancing over his shoulder.

Svetlana turned to see the crew from downstairs, now wielding a wider variety of bladed weapons and ranged out on the deck, rather than constricted in a hallway. She drew her pistol and aimed it at the one she'd slashed earlier. Then she paused and aimed it down the hole they'd just climbed out of. "We're going to be leaving you in just a moment, and we won't bother you again. But if you take even one step toward us, I've got a clean line on your boiler. Would be a pity if that sprung a leak."

The crew of *The Flaming Pony* remained where they were standing, several of them looking to the crew member who had been in front. He shouted toward the hole. "Buck? Close up the panel."

The wooden panel slid back into place, blending seamlessly with the deck on this side. But Svetlana still knew where the hole had been, and her aim didn't waver.

"You think a couple of inches of wood is going to stop a bullet?"

"Naw, but it might redirect it," the man replied.

A rush of wind ruffled Svetlana's short hair, covering her good eye with a veil of darkness and making her just as blind in that eye

6

as she was in her other. She held her hands up. "Like I said, we're going now." Without even looking, she spun and vaulted over the rail of *The Flaming Pony*. Her heels struck wood, and she let out a breath. The moment she heard Athos and Indigo hit the deck as well, she shouted, "Jo, hard right. Get us out of here before they find their cannon."

*The Silent Monsoon* rocked to the right and downward, and was away from *The Flaming Pony* in a flash.

Athos shook his head. "Yeah, that's the last time I'm going on a 'supply run.'"

Svetlana gave him a crooked smile as she pulled off her monocular, the brass and glass contraption that normally covered her blind right eye, giving her the smallest amount of vision on that side of her body. "What, too old for this nonsense?"

"Look who's talking," he quipped back. "I'm just considering your advanced age."

Svetlana smirked. "Oh yes, my thirty-seven long years on this earth. We should think about retiring."

"That'll be the day."

~

"What is all of that junk?" Jo grumbled as she surveyed the piles of loot that Indigo had scattered across the mess table.

Indigo pointed to objects in turn. "Ionic buffers, a non-linear velocity accelerator, all-weather adhesion bolts—"

"Pretend I didn't ask," Jo said with a chuckle. "More important, did you get anything to help fix that steering glitch we picked up after Bonebriar?"

Indigo blinked a few times at Jo, shook his head, and returned to sorting his haul.

It had been less than a month since Svetlana and her crew had located the virtually unknown island of Bonebriar, which had been stricken from Republic maps since the island's inhabitants had left the Republic years previous. The crew had gone there in search of information about a missing cask of Cranglimmering whiskey, which had led them to pieces of a map, hidden amongst the staves of the seven casks of Cranglimmering, that was purported to lead to the Last Emperor's Hoard, a long-lost treasure. Key to that treasure was the Gem of the Seas, which allowed its bearer to control the oceans. Since the oceans had begun boiling at the same time the treasure was lost, even the most skeptical could not help but believe the two events were related.

Drassilis was an automaton they had encountered on Bonebriar, along with his creator, Dr. Vertiline Dowhty, also known as Lady Elinor de Whittvy. Lady de Whittvy had been both a brilliant scientist and an infamous thief, until she had met her demise at the hands of an overzealous Air Fleet ensign. Her creation, Drassilis, had been deactivated due to damage he had sustained shortly before Lady de Whittvy died, and now Svetlana and her crew were engaged in trying to reactivate him to learn what additional information he might have about the map or the hoard.

Turning Indigo to face her, Svetlana asked, "Okay, Indy. What else do you need to get him back up and running?"

He shrugged.

"Then get started, and if you need anything, call up to the bridge. All you're working on until it's done is Drassilis, got it?"

Indigo nodded, his blue hair bouncing around his thin face as he did.

Jo leaned toward Svetlana and whispered, "So, who's on Indy watch until he's done?"

"We'll take turns," Svetlana said. "Annette said she'd cover the first shift."

"Aw, that's kind of you, Doc," Jo said, grinning as Annette clambered down the stairs, book in hand.

Annette looked up, the skin around her dark eyes crinkling as she smiled. "Hey, I get to sit in the mess, drink tea, read, and make sure Indy eats? I'll take it. Anyway, what else is there for me to do?"

"At the moment, there's not much for any of us to do," Svetlana said. "We don't know where to look for any of the other casks. I'm not even sure that Drassilis will have any information that we don't already, but he's our best lead so far, what with Lady de Whittvy being dead and all." She sighed, trying not to think too much about the woman who had captured her attention on Bonebriar. Svetlana regretted not knowing if their burgeoning friendship might have grown into something more. "At least there's a chance we can revive the automaton."

Annette looked over the table and let out a long whistle. "You got all of this on *The Flaming Pony*?"

"Yeah. One-stop shopping."

Annette arched an eyebrow. "Shopping?"

With a shrug, Svetlana said, "I threw their mechanic a couple of Quinpence."

"Why'd you go and do a thing like that?" Jo asked, frowning deeply.

"It's not like I paid what these parts are worth," Svetlana spat back. "Regardless, I don't see any reason to go and make more enemies if we can help it. We're already between a sandbar and a coral reef, what with being on the wrong side of the Air Fleet."

"But we're on Mayor Kavisoli's good side," Jo said, crossing her arms over her chest. "Even better, if you take the job. Right, Doc?"

Annette glanced between Svetlana and Jo, but nodded slowly. "Jo's right, Captain. Working for Mayor Kavisoli would mean steady income and at least some protection from the Air Fleet."

"Fully aware," Svetlana said, turning her attention from Jo to Annette. "But you know my reasons."

"I do, but you said it yourself. We have nothing else to do at the moment, except wait for Indy to fix Drassilis—"

"Oops." Indigo's voice cut through Annette's, drawing the attention of all three of the women.

"Oops?" Svetlana asked, entering the mess and approaching where Indigo had the automaton sprawled out on the floor.

"Missing parts."

Annette crouched beside Indigo and grimaced. "Cover that up."

Svetlana craned her neck to allow her good eye to see what Annette was talking about. She saw only a flash of what looked like bloodied flesh before Annette closed Drassilis's chest plate. The crew wasn't entirely certain how the automaton worked, but it seemed that he had both mechanical and organic parts. Though normally Drassilis was dressed in fine clothing, Indigo had stripped the automaton down to just his metal casing and whatever lurked inside. With articulated eyelids closed on his emotionless filigree face, Drassilis appeared to be resting, rather than deactivated.

"We don't need to make him move, Indy. We need his brain to work again," Annette chided softly.

"I know," Indigo said. "But I got pieces for moving too."

Annette nodded. "Brain first. Moving second. Do you have the right pieces for his brain?"

"Yes. No. Maybe. I don't know."

Svetlana crouched beside Indigo. "Okay, Indy. Explain it to me."

"All the pieces are still in his brain," Indigo began, though he looked at Svetlana sidelong as he did. "But there's no oomph in his brain."

"So he needs oomph," Svetlana suggested.

"Yeah."

Jo joined the group on the floor and traced a line above Drassilis's still body from his head to his chest. "And you want the oomph to come from his heart ... place ... thing." She looked at Svetlana and Annette. "Whatever makes him run."

"Yeah. But it's broken. And I don't have heart parts."

"Then we need to find Drassilis a new heart," Svetlana said with a smile, rising from her crouch. Her joints complained as she did. She had thought that an increase in her activity level, since she'd been sharing Lar's bed, would make her body less stiff, but every morning, she seemed to find a new ache or pain. She didn't want to face the fact that she was nearing forty, and she certainly didn't want her crew to think she was getting old, even if she and Athos joked about it.

Annette peered up at Svetlana. "That's not as easy as you think, Svetlana."

"I know it's not," Svetlana replied. "But I don't think it has to be an actual heart. Just a little engine, right?"

Indigo nodded vigorously. "A little engine." He rose and began sketching on the mess table with a piece of charcoal before anyone could stop him. He drew a rough sketch of Drassilis, and then marked three spots—the head, the chest, and the waist. "Three little engines. One to make the brain go, one to make the wheels go, and one to tie them together."

"Perfect," Svetlana said. "So can you build those?"

"Yes." Indigo nodded again, then shook his head. "But not with the pieces I have. I need more gears."

Svetlana looked at the parts strewn across the floor and table. "What, there aren't gears here?"

"Not the right gears," Indigo replied.

She sighed. "Alright, where can we get the gears you need?"

"Heliopolis?"

Svetlana, Annette, and Jo all shook their heads in unison. Heliopolis had been their home base previously, but it was also the

10

headquarters of the Air Fleet, and the entire crew of *The Silent Monsoon* had been added to the Air Fleet's most wanted list after Bonebriar.

"Not an option, kiddo," Jo said. "Sorry. It's too hot for us there."

Indigo frowned, brow furrowed. "Then somewhere else."

"Maybe one of Lar's people will have an idea where to find gears," Svetlana suggested.

Annette looked at Svetlana and smiled. "Back to Rrusadon, then?"

"May as well," Svetlana said, relaxing her shoulders as she spoke. She didn't want to continue the argument about whether she should accept Lar's offer to make her head of the Rrusadon Port Authority. Not while she wasn't in a position to make up her mind about it, at least. "I'm sure he'll be happy to have us back for a while."

Jo rolled her eyes and smirked. "And you won't complain much either."

"Hey, happy captain, happy crew."

# CHAPTER TWO

The foliage covering Rrusadon's platform had once been a deterrent, but now the lush green was a welcome sight, the loamy scent in the air a welcome smell that covered up the standard sulfurous smell on most platform cities kept aloft by geysers. Rrusadon, home to the Kavisoli family, had become *The Silent Monsoon*'s second home. Once upon a time, Svetlana would have resisted throwing in their lot with a crime family that had bought a seat in the Republican Senate, but Larson Kavisoli, the newly appointed Mayor of Rrusadon, had proven to be a trusted ally. The fact that she and Lar had discovered a mutual attraction was just an added benefit.

"Oh. Look." Jo gave an empty dock space at the public dock a pointed look. "Our usual space is open. Like Lar said it would be," Jo said. She pulled the cord to sound a whistle, a new addition to their docking process. On the ground at Rrusadon, the docking crew scrambled to action, ready to guide the ship onto the docking struts and lash it into place.

It was a lot more civilized than the docks at Heliopolis, where crews had to deploy from their own ships in order to dock. But Svetlana's gaze still slid over a nearby private docking platform with only a handful of ships docked there. Another ship was under construction, Rrusadon being one of the rare places in the Republic with the natural resources available for new construction from wood. It was the beginning of the Rrusadon fleet.

Lar had offered Svetlana a position as the admiral of Rrusadon's Port Authority. Accepting it would ensure that she and her crew wanted for nothing, with the steady work it would provide all of them. And it would guarantee *The Silent Monsoon* a docking slip on the private platform. But Svetlana was hesitant. Most everyone on

Rrusadon seemed to know that she came and went from the Mayor's house as she pleased, and it wasn't much of a secret that she was there as Lar's companion. Which was why she hesitated over his job offer.

She worried about someone telling the Air Fleet where they could find her. She'd broken most of her ties with her former comrades at the Fleet, which gave them all the more motivation to bring her in. Though Lar assured her that no one living on Rrusadon would assist in such a thing, Svetlana was all too familiar with the allure of money. If the Air Fleet offered enough of a price on her head, even the might of the Kavisoli family couldn't keep her safe.

She also didn't want the reputation that Lar had offered her the job to keep her around. So far, their relationship had been a novelty for Svetlana. She wasn't accustomed to being pursued— she was more likely to be the one in pursuit of a potential love interest—but Lar had continued to shower her with affection. She found that she enjoyed his attentions.

Breaking her from her reverie, Athos asked, "What's the plan, then?"

Svetlana pulled herself back to the here and now, though she felt her ears burning still with her thoughts of her most recent dalliances with Lar. "We need to see if the engineers here have some of the small gears that Indy says he needs to repair Drassilis."

"All of us?" Athos asked, his gaze flickering toward Jo.

"No," Svetlana said. "Indy and I can handle it if you've got something else in mind."

Athos shrugged. "Maybe later. For now, I'm still trying to get gossip from Heliopolis, but the airwave messages don't allow for much nuance."

"Nuance?" Jo grumbled. "Don't you mean 'flirting'?" Though she and Athos had an on-again, off-again, relationship, she complained about his constant flirting disguised as "gossip," regardless of their current status.

"Do you think anyone on Heliopolis will know where the other casks are?" Annette asked, drowning out any further complaints from Jo.

With a lazy shrug, Athos said, "I'm certain someone there does. It's just figuring out who and how to contact them when I can't speak with my usual sources."

Jo rolled her eyes. "I hear there are lips involved, but I hardly think that's 'speaking' that you'd be doing."

"I'm willing to give what it takes," Athos said with a shrug.

"Then I'll come with you to the airwave office," Annette said. "See if we can't find a way to add some nuance to as few words as possible."

Giving Athos a pointed glare, Jo said, "Well, if everyone else is running off, I suppose I can go make some money. Lar's got a new bunch of pilots he wants me to train. And he pays a lot better than sitting around and waiting."

Svetlana nodded, checking her pocket watch, which had been a gift from Lar. "Next Lift is in an hour, so back here after two Lifts?" Due to the regular eruptions of the geysers that held the platform city aloft, nearly every city told their time based on the intervals between Lifts. Traveling between platform cities complicated the matter substantially, as different geysers had different cycles of activity. The watch Lar had given Svetlana was perfectly accurate on Rrusadon, but had to be recalibrated if they spent any significant amount of time in another location.

The crew nodded and headed their separate ways. Svetlana descended to the mess, where Indigo now had wires draped across most of the room. "Indy? We're here. Grab those little engines."

"Can't."

"What? Why not?" Peering through the tangled wires, Svetlana couldn't see Indigo anywhere in the room.

"Trying something new."

"I thought you needed gears," Svetlana said as she pushed aside enough of the wires to make her way into the room. Some of the wires ran through pulleys on the ceiling that hadn't been there before. Tracing their route, she found some attached to the tea pan on the cook stove, and the smell of burning peat told her that the stove was on.

"Indy, what are you doing? You don't want water to short all of this out."

"Not water. Steam bulbs."

"Steam bulbs still use water!"

"I took it out first." A crackling sound caused Indigo to glance into the pan, and his eyes grew wide. "Oops."

Svetlana winced as she thought about the steam bulbs shattering in the tea pan. She rushed toward the stove, her arm shielding her good eye as best she could while still seeing where she was going, and lifted the pan off the cook stove. The surfaces of the steam bulbs had a spider web of cracks across their surface, but they still appeared to be intact. Glancing at the wires again, she carefully extracted them from the tea pan, leaving them dangling from the pulleys on the ceiling. "Toss me a towel?"

Indigo brushed past her back and began rummaging around in the cupboards. "Clean or dirty?"

"It really doesn't matter, Indy," Svetlana said. A faint tinkling sound came from the pan. "Whichever you find first is fine."

Indigo pressed something soft into Svetlana's hand, and she draped it across the top of the tea pan, which she then moved to the countertop. Then she took a deep breath, certain that even if the steam bulbs shattered now, she and Indigo would not be hit with flying glass shards.

"Okay, do you have a list of what gears we need to get from the Mayor's engineers?" Svetlana asked, finally looking at Indigo.

Indigo frowned. "In my head. But he's full of secrets."

Once she made sense of what Indigo was saying, Svetlana nodded. "Yes, Drassilis is full of secrets. But I can't have you bursting all our steam bulbs trying to get him back up and running. Maybe you can get the extra hands you wanted now. How does that sound?" Svetlana didn't cherish the idea of bringing in outsiders to help get Drassilis repaired, but at least she could be sure that no one directly related to Lar would sell them out to the Air Fleet, which was the amount of trustworthiness she needed at the moment.

Indigo surveyed the large knotted oak table and shook his head. "There's nowhere to put all this."

Svetlana crossed her arms over her chest. "But if we don't move it, then where are we going to eat tonight?"

Indigo frowned. "It's going to take a long time."

"Probably so, Indy. You should have thought of that before you made this mess." She immediately regretted her statement, as it sounded exactly like something her grandmother had told her many times while she was growing up. Rubbing her hand across her face, she said, "I'm sorry, that was unkind. I'll talk to the Mayor later, and see if he can send someone here to help you. But I still want to be able to eat dinner on the table tonight. Understand?"

"Okay," Indigo said glumly. "I'll clean off the table."

"And the floor. And the rafters. All of it."

"Okay, all of it."

~

Svetlana leaned back in her chair on the bridge, looking out at the fluffy white clouds in the distance. It was rare that the ship was so quiet, and she was trying to enjoy it. She wasn't good at relaxing, but she took a deep breath, letting it out slowly. She felt a little calmer, and she breathed in to try again.

The door to the bridge slamming open disrupted the silence. Ready to yell at Indigo or Jo, Svetlana turned and instead frowned when she saw Annette.

Annette's cheeks shone pink through her dark brown skin, her breathing rapid. "Where's the film that Lady de Whittvy made?" Annette gasped.

Svetlana rose and looked around the bridge for the film. The thin celluloid sheet, created by Lady de Whittvy, contained much of her research into a variety of fields, including at least a portion of the map that the crew of *The Silent Monsoon* was attempting to complete. "Did you run all the way from the airwave office?"

Annette nodded, still working to catch her breath. She took the film from Svetlana and turned it in several directions before she found what she was looking for. Then she dropped the film onto the command console in the center of the room and pointed to something that looked like a fragment of a word. Leaning closer to it, she said, "No, wait. Is that it?"

"Is what what?" Svetlana asked. Despite the many years she and Annette had spent working together, beginning when Svetlana and Annette's late husband, Jack, had served in the same Air Fleet unit, Svetlana still couldn't read the doctor's mind.

Pausing to take a deep breath, Annette said, "Okay, I went to the airwave office with Athos, like we planned. And we were talking to the operator there, and she said something about the way that the transmissions come through that reminded me of something on the film. Or at least something I thought I had seen." She shook her head. "I've been over this whole thing hundreds of times, it feels like. And I haven't made any more progress on it than the day we got it."

"Well, Indy's trying to get Drassilis back up and running, assuming he doesn't blow himself up before that happens."

"Did I miss something exciting?"

"Drained steam bulbs, in the tea pan, on the cook stove, while it was on." Svetlana shook her head. "We may want to give the pan a good scrub to make sure all the glass shards are out before we make tea. And maybe wear boots in the mess for a few days."

Annette gasped. "He's alright, though?"

"As well as he ever is. Lost my temper with him, so he's probably smarting from that. I sounded like my grandmother."

With a soft chuckle, Annette said, "Ouch. Bet you're smarting too."

Svetlana nodded. "Were you ever a wild and crazy teenager, or were you just born straight into a doctor's coat?"

"Neither," Annette said with a shrug. "Going into medicine was my rebellion."

Shaking her head again, Svetlana smiled. "So whatever you thought you saw on the film—"

"It's not the same," Annette said, pointing to the portion of the film she was talking about. "The airwave operator said that things come in as pulses, right? And those pulses are translated into letters. It's all translated by machine now, but there's an underlying code, and the woman there drew me a picture of what it looks like. But it's much less jagged than what's on the film."

Svetlana squinted at the film, allowing the image to blur. "But if we smoothed out the edges of it? Could it be a letter or a word?"

"Maybe. It could just be a design. Or a circuit. Or maybe Lady de Whittvy just needed to make sure whatever sort of pen she used to make this was still working." Annette shrugged as she sunk into one of the chairs on the bridge. "Most of this film is outside of my expertise. We've had a dozen different people look at it, and any one of us can pick out certain parts that we understand. There's no one who's understood all of it. No one."

Svetlana nodded as she took a seat across from Annette. "Vertiline—Lady de Whittvy—was a singular woman."

"She was a super genius if she understood all of this. This is ... it's multiple lifetimes worth of study."

"Maybe for you or me," Svetlana said with a chuckle. "But I know I'm horrible about studying. I only learned what I needed to pass my exams and keep a boat in the air when I was at the Academy."

Annette stretched her arms out, then brought them back to comb through her hair. "Ugh, don't remind me about the Academy. Bobby made it pretty clear that you're no longer wanted there, so good riddance to the lot of them. But it's a shame—I know half a dozen experts there who could help decipher this. Too bad they'd sell us out just as soon as we contacted any of them, even on an academic matter."

"Even if we weren't wanted, I don't think I trust the Air Fleet with this information," Svetlana said, her voice taking on a more somber note. "In fact, I'd say there's good odds that they're trying to track down the casks as well."

"To the same end as us?" Annette asked.

"If the Gem of the Seas really does what they say it does? Definitely. Why wouldn't the Republic want to control the oceans, like the Empire did centuries ago?"

Annette nodded, rising and considering the film for a long moment before she spoke again. "Do you miss him?"

Svetlana knew who Annette referred to, but still asked, "Who?"

"Bobby."

Rear Admiral Robert Beauregard had been Svetlana's mentor when she was a part of the Air Fleet. She counted herself among a select few whom the wizened officer had befriended to a point of allowing them to call him Bobby, but recent events had shattered their close relationship, culminating in the Air Fleet's callous disregard for the citizens of Bonebriar, Lady de Whittvy's former home. With a shrug, Svetlana replied, "Now and then. But he made it pretty clear that he didn't really care about us the way we cared about him. It's in the past, and we have to move on."

Annette nodded. "The problem is figuring out where exactly moving on should take us next."

~

Svetlana strode up the steps to Lar's house. It was the nicest home on Rrusadon, but Svetlana knew that was just for show. Lar was comfortable in whatever circumstances life threw at him. Neither his private study nor his rooms were half as ostentatious as his house. Svetlana preferred those private areas of the house to the formality of the public-facing areas, but she was learning to navigate both.

She flashed a friendly smile at the young woman behind the reception desk. Like most of the women who made Rrusadon their home, the woman was olive-skinned with dark hair. Unlike many of those women, however, Lar's secretary Celeste wore blouses and skirts reminiscent of Republic fashions rather than the garments that looked more like remnants that had been trimmed from someone else's clothing construction, which seemed to be the fashion of most of Rrusadon's inhabitants. "Good afternoon, Celeste. Could you please let the Mayor know that I'd like to speak with him?"

"He's available now, Captain," Celeste replied, her smile both genuine and teasing.

Svetlana glanced back at the main entry hall, a high-ceilinged room of columns painted to look like gold-veined marble with a few backless crimson velvet seats strewn about. Several other people waited in these seats or paced the room, their footsteps echoing off the stone floor. "What about these people?" she asked Celeste in a low voice.

Celeste shrugged. "He told me that if you came in, I should bump you to the top." She glanced down at the ledger on her desk. "He should be just finishing up in the pool."

"Oh." Svetlana knew that Lar meant well, but she chafed at the thought of him giving his staff special instructions related to her. But no matter how many times she told him this, he continued to give her a higher priority than his citizens. "Perhaps I'll just wait," she said.

"If you insist," Celeste said, jotting down Svetlana's name in another part of the ledger. "Ah, he also wanted me to ask if you're available for dinner this evening?"

"He couldn't ask me that himself?" Svetlana murmured under her breath. Aloud, she said, "I might be. It's related to what I need to speak to him about."

Celeste smiled and made a small mark in her ledger book.

The awkward silence broke when Lar's booming voice called out, "Celeste?"

Celeste smiled at Svetlana as she rose.

Svetlana followed Celeste a few steps and saw Lar, dressed in a bulky white dressing gown. Its v-shaped neckline highlighted both his olive skin and his well-muscled chest. He inclined his head to the side, looking past Celeste to arch an eyebrow in Svetlana's direction and give her a flirtatious smile, still damp clumps of long brown hair falling over his shoulder, and Svetlana could not help but grin. He was handsome and charming, and she still felt butterflies in her stomach when he smiled at her like that.

"Why is she waiting?" Lar asked Celeste, just loud enough for Svetlana to hear.

"She insisted," Celeste replied.

Lar leaned to the side and looked at Svetlana again, shaking his head as he did. "Send the rest of them away."

Celeste nodded before returning to the entry hall. "Mayor Kavisoli will send his personal secretary to meet with each of you shortly," she announced to the waiting crowd. Then she caught Svetlana's good eye and inclined her head toward Lar, still waiting in the hallway.

Svetlana frowned but slipped past Celeste and followed Lar to his office.

"You know I hate it when you do that," Lar said as he opened the door to his private study."

Svetlana feigned ignorance. "Do what?" They'd danced these steps before, but she wasn't about to acquiesce to Lar's utter disregard for protocol when it came to her.

"Try to wait in line like you need to petition for a sliver of my time," he said, leaning in for a kiss.

Svetlana only kissed him delicately at first, but her grumpiness over his behavior melted away as their lips met. In an instant, her fingers were woven into his damp hair, and he had wrapped his arms around her waist and shoulders, pulling her close as their kisses grew more intense.

When they finally paused for a breath, Lar still kept his arms around Svetlana, and she moved her hands down to touch his shoulders. The dressing gown had slipped from one of his shoulders, and she traced a lazy line from the nape of his neck to his bicep.

"Now then, we are both busy people." He paused to kiss her again, lightly this time, as though he were teasing her, and continued to end each of his sentences with a kiss. "I know you only come here during business hours when you have important matters to discuss. I also know that if I cannot see you when you arrive, you'll find something else to drag you away before I see you."

Svetlana leaned into Lar's final kiss, taking a moment to savor the warmth of his soft lips and the clean scent of his beard after his swim. Her hand slid lower on his arm, and he began to extract his arm from his sleeve, as though he would remove his dressing gown entirely right there in his office, if that was what she wanted. Letting out a deep sigh, she pulled back from kissing him, and said, "You're right, I do have business."

Taking a step back and adjusting his dressing gown, Lar asked, "Is it an answer to my offer?"

"Not yet," she replied. "I need to borrow an engineer—one of your family members—to help Indy with Drassilis. Preferably someone who's fond of a clean workroom and might instill that same virtue in a teenaged boy."

"That's easily done." He sat at his desk and began to write a note. "Anything else, my dear Sveta?"

"Have your people found anything more on the remaining casks?"

He shook his head. "Lord Mayor Silver is still missing, along with his family and personal staff. We can only assume that they are the only ones who know the location of his cask. I've had no response from the Gyrfalcons or Lady Mayor Somerset." He shrugged. "Old money versus new, I suppose. Still no word on the Bartram Cask, then?"

"Not until we get Drassilis back up and running, I fear. Indy has a plan for that, but he needs some help, if you've got some to spare."

Lar smiled. "Then let me finish this note and send it off. Then, perhaps, we should adjourn to my quarters." He arched an eyebrow at her. "Unless there's more to discuss?"

Svetlana pinched at her lower lip, trying to hide a smile, and resisting the urge to drag Lar to his quarters before the note was written. "Nothing more that we need words for, but there was something about dinner?"

"Oh, yes. Would you prefer to dine first?"

Svetlana allowed the smile to surface now. "No, dinner after, I think. Though it depends entirely on whether your engineer can get Indy's project out of our mess before dinner time."

"Hmm, then perhaps I should delay in sending this note," Lar said, waving the paper in front of him.

"Not unless your invitation is extended to my whole crew." Before he could respond, there was a knock at the door.

"Yes?" Lar growled, frowning.

"Sorry to disturb your meeting, Mayor," Celeste called from the other side of the door. "We've just had an airwave from Heliopolis. There's an Air Fleet delegation en route."

# CHAPTER THREE

Several of Rrusadon's dock workers poked their heads out of the small shed at the edge of the of dock, where *The Silent Monsoon* was moored, in response to Svetlana's rapid footsteps as she ran toward the ship.

"Air Fleet inbound! Could we get some help going incognito?"

Immediately, the dock workers emerged and boarded the ship. A moment later, the rose balloon, a brilliant red small balloon that was Svetlana's one nod to vanity when it came to the appearance of her ship, began to descend. A pair of dock workers with their pale skin reddened by time spent in the sun began spreading a large oilcloth across the prow of the boat, obscuring the name of the ship and providing a place where the rose balloon could be hidden away.

Svetlana nodded at them as she ran up the gangplank. "Good work. Let's get oilcloths all around. Make it look like we're renovating."

"More oilcloths?" one of the female dock workers, this one with pink undertones to her dark brown skin, asked.

"We don't know who is on those Air Fleet ships. If it's the Rear Admiral, or any of several other high-ranking officers, they might recognize the *Monsoon* even if we cover up her name. Use bedsheets if we have to." Svetlana shoved open the door to the bridge, which was empty. Kneeling down behind the wheel, she lifted a small brass plate and bellowed into the hole it covered. "Athos, Annette, I need you topside."

After a few minutes of pacing the bridge, Svetlana picked up a spyglass and trained it on the sky in the direction of Heliopolis. No ships hovered there yet, but she suspected it wouldn't be long before she and the others would be able to pick out details of the Air Fleet vessels that approached.

Annette slipped through the door at the back of the bridge first. Taking in the dock workers moving around outside, she asked, "What's going on?"

"Lar got an airwave. He's expecting an Air Fleet delegation. No sense of why, but we're not taking any chances."

"Do you think they've caught wind that we've been spending time here?" Annette asked.

"Hopefully that's not the case. But I'm not taking any chances on them suddenly realizing where we've been hiding."

Athos strolled in through the main bridge door. "Who's on their way?"

"We don't know yet, other than Air Fleet," Svetlana replied. She raised the spyglass again. Living her entire life with only one working eye had given her fairly good vision in it, which was only enhanced by the spyglass. While others might complain about losing their depth perception while looking through such a device, she had never had any depth perception to lose.

Far in the distance, Svetlana made out two ships, but they were still miles away from landing at Rrusadon. "Only two," she said.

"Then they're probably not coming for you," Athos said, gesturing for the spyglass. "They'd send at least a dozen if they wanted to make sure we didn't get away." He lifted the spyglass to his right eye and frowned. "I don't think they're even sending anyone above a Lieutenant on those ships."

"So diplomatic escort?" Annette asked. "Didn't you all get sent on a bunch of runs like that straight out of the Academy?"

"Athos did," Svetlana said. "I just tagged along for the fun of it, most of the time." She paused and frowned. "Okay, but if it's just low-ranking officers, then it's not anyone who's going to know us. Might not even be anyone who's heard the rumors that we're here."

"Or it could be someone sent to confirm the rumors," Athos said, handing the spyglass back to Svetlana. "I'll find something appropriate to wear and go be one of the Mayor's hangers-on for a few hours."

"No, that's not a good idea," Svetlana said. "If it does turn out to be someone we know, then they'll recognize you straight away. And then they'll assume I'm here too, and Jo as well. We're better off staying on the ship. Lar will send someone to let us know if we need to get away for a bit." Svetlana stiffened as she mentally located each member of her crew. "Is Jo still training the Kavisoli pilots?"

Athos whirled, wide-eyed. "I don't know. She wasn't back when we got back, was she, Annette?"

"No, we got grounded as soon as we got word that Air Fleet was on their way," Jo said as she pushed open the hatch that accessed the bridge from below decks. "So I got back here as fast as I could. By the way, tell Lar that his dock crews need to work on their knots. They left a lot of loose ropes hanging. Anyone could shimmy up one of those on the back side of the ship and crawl through a window."

Svetlana tensed. "Was there any indication that anyone has been on the ship that way?"

"Well, me," Jo said with a shrug. "But other people could have."

"We need to check the ship over," Svetlana said. "This looks diplomatic, but if the Air Fleet sent an advance scout to see if we're here, they might think they can catch us unaware."

Athos shook his head. "They wouldn't have sent an airwave if they wanted to surprise us."

Svetlana clenched her fists. "Okay, probably not. Nonetheless, let's check the ship, stem to stern. If we don't find anything, then we wait until Lar has news for us. Anyone know where Indy is?"

"He's still in the mess," Annette said, "and it's still a disaster in there."

"Yeah, Lar didn't have time to send someone over to help with that yet, I suppose. Alright, Jo and Annette, check below. Athos and I will check up here and see if we can figure anything else out from what we can see when they get nearer."

Annette and Jo nodded and slipped back through the hatch in the floor of the bridge.

"If someone snuck on board, they won't be on deck," Athos said.

"I realize that, but they might have left some sign of their passing." She left the bridge through the main door, Athos close behind her. "If the Air Fleet didn't send a scout to find us, then why are they coming here now?"

"Well, you were found in Lar's room when Narci showed up to arrest him, so you've got ties to him. Might just be that they're finally getting around to seeing what he knows. They might have sent people who are good at ferreting out information."

"Lar is too smart for that," Svetlana scoffed.

"Then they could be offering him something that would get him to sell you out."

"He won't," Svetlana snapped.

"I'm glad you trust him," Athos said, taking Svetlana's hands in his. "Truly, it's a good look on you. But many people don't trust a Kavisoli, and the Air Fleet may be counting on that distrust, especially since they don't know about your relationship with him. If I had to speculate, I'd say they're on a fact-finding mission. See if they can spot us. See if Lar knows your whereabouts. See if he'll sell you out for a high enough price. That all makes sense, right?"

Svetlana released some of the tension from her shoulders. "Yeah, okay. That makes sense. And if they're not sending anyone higher than a Lieutenant, then we know it's not Bobby or Narci."

"See," Athos said. "At least we've got that working in our favor."

"So you say," Svetlana grumbled.

~

A knock on Svetlana's cabin door halted her pacing. None of the crew had found any sign that anyone other than them and the Rrusadon dock workers had been on board their ship, but she was still worried about what it meant that the Air Fleet had sent a message preceding two ships. "What?"

"Note from Lar," Annette said. "The messenger said it was important."

Scrambling for the door, Svetlana nonetheless tried to look calm when she opened it. She smiled at Annette and took the note.

*Come to the house, but dress like staff. I've insisted on no conversation here until after dinner.-L*

Her brow creased as she reread the note. "We're going to need some of that ridiculous glitter that the staff at Lar's wears."

"Ah, that explains the box, then," Annette said, handing a small package to Svetlana. "But when you say we, I do hope you're not including me."

28

"You'll look better with this stuff on than I will," Svetlana grumbled. Calling down the hallway, she shouted, "Jo, I think I'm gonna need your help."

A moment later, Jo popped her head out of her room, long auburn hair tousled. "What for?"

"Dressing up like servant girls to go listen to the conversation between Lar and Air Fleet, it seems."

"Ooh, pick me," Athos said from within Jo's room.

Jo's face vanished back into her room, followed by an "oof" from Athos. Then Jo returned to the door. "You're gonna need a veil or something to cover up your eyes."

Svetlana nodded. "One of these days, I get to pick the ridiculous costumes. I can only handle so much of you two dressing me." Opening the box, Svetlana grimaced. "Oh, never mind. Lar sent clothes too." She picked up a thin band of fabric and shook her head. "If this can actually be called clothes."

"Technically yes, though I don't like it much more than you do," Jo said as she shucked off her trousers and stuck a pale leg into the hallway. "I'm gonna need a whole lot of glitter."

"I hate glitter," Svetlana grumbled.

~

An hour later, Svetlana and Jo stood outside of the drawing room where Lar's other staff members had led them. Annette had located an old hat with a veil that she had saved from her mourning days, which they had wrapped with enough gold ribbon to make it fit the theme.

"So all you need to do is pour drinks when you go in and watch to add more if they begin to get empty," Dionara, the ebony-skinned serving girl who had just come out of the drawing room, explained. Her short black hair had gold highlights on some of the tight curls, and she wore the customary glitter across her skin with unearthly grace. "It's simple."

"How empty is empty?" Jo asked. Her lips drew into a tight line, pale beneath the layers of gold makeup she had applied to the rest of her face.

Dionara shrugged. "You get a sense for it. If they raise their glass and there's not much left, slip up next to them and refill it."

Jo's frown deepened. "But, what if they raise their glass and there's still a lot in it? Or what if they raise their glass, and you start to pour, but then they move their glass?"

Svetlana laid her hand on Jo's arm. "Give me the bottle. Have you never been to any sort of society function?"

"Not for a very long time. And I certainly wasn't paying attention to the servants, or how frequently they refilled the drinks."

Dionara arched one of her eyebrows, her lips a firm line. "You should probably have watched more closely if you wanted to consider yourself a talented spy."

"She's right." Svetlana gave Dionara a quick nod, trying to let her expression apologize for Jo's rude obliviousness. "Just follow my lead," she said as she pushed open the drawing room door.

Inside, a thick, acrid cloud hung in the small room, emanating from cigars in half the hands in the room. The haze made it difficult to determine who was there, but Lar's voice was clear as day. "Ah, more drinks? Excellent idea." He winked at Svetlana. "Perhaps some fresh air as well?"

Svetlana nudged Jo in the direction of the windows, and the pilot scooted away to open them while Svetlana made her way around the room with the bottle Dionara had given her. If she'd had her way, she might have dropped some sort of soporific into the bottle before serving it, but she knew Lar would not want the Air Fleet officers to stay overnight, under any circumstances.

As she stopped in front of each officer, she ran a practiced eye over each of their nameplates and ranks. Lieutenant Gurneel, Lieutenant Torrum, Lieutenant Junior Grade Makron, Ensign Grimault, and Ensign Roenn. Only the first and last were men, while the other three were all women. And it was just as Athos has expected—no one higher than a Lieutenant.

Lieutenant Gurneel was a raven-haired gentleman with crows' feet at the corners of his eyes, the wrinkles laying across his pale skin like bleached old leather. The lack of silver in his hair suggested to Svetlana that either he dyed it, or that his skin falsely gave him more years than he truly had, and his rank suggested that he'd spent most of his time behind a desk rather than on a ship. He smiled up at Svetlana as she refilled his glass, but no recognition showed in his coal-black eyes. His voice was possessed of a slow drawl when he spoke. "So, Mayor, is this the legendary Cranglimmering?"

Lar chuckled. "I'm afraid not even I have access to Cranglimmering. My family's wealth provides me with much to be envied, but some things cannot be bought at any price."

"I misspoke," Gurneel continued. "The synthetic Cranglimmering that your chemists are said to have created."

"Ah, no. Alas, the trial run did not pass muster. I'm afraid it's back to the drawing board for us."

"I wonder, though," Lieutenant Junior Grade Makron began, flipping a pale blonde braid over her shoulder, "where did your chemists start on such an impressive project?" She watched Lar closely, one long finger tapping her nearly imperceptible thin, lips, almost as pale as her hair.

Lar shrugged. "There's always been such a fuss about Cranglimmering that I had to see what it was all about."

"I heard a rumor that there was a sample of Cranglimmering that they were working from," Makron said. "Any truth to that?"

"I feel as though I'm being interviewed, Lieutenant," Lar said, smiling broadly. "Where are you going with this?"

Lieutenant Torrum, an older woman who looked dimly familiar to Svetlana, held out a hand in front of Makron's chest. She, too, had the leathery skin of a long-term Fleet officer, with piercing green eyes that gazed out from her weathered brown face. But her hair held more strands of silver than black, and her hand bore a few faint liver spots. "Now Mayor, you must understand that the Air Fleet is still assisting the Heliopolis Port Authority in their investigation of the disappearance of the Bartram Cask. We're just following up on that."

Hearing Torrum's voice triggered Svetlana's memory of her. Torrum, despite her advanced age, had begun at the Academy at the same time as Svetlana had, and they had both been among the group who was denied pilot training, though in Torrum's case it was because of some sort of balance issue.

A cold sweat broke out on Svetlana's brow, beneath the borrowed hat and veil. It had been a mistake to think that she could pose as a serving girl at Lar's house while there was Air Fleet here. She moved toward Jo and handed the pilot the bottle. "I need to get out of here," Svetlana murmured.

Before Jo responded, Lar answered Torrum, "Oh, of course, I understand. But alas, I know nothing about the Bartram Cask—" He hesitated, though Svetlana dared not turn around to see why. "Some thought it might have been stolen as a gift to me, on the occasion of my inauguration, but I can assure you, I have not laid eyes on that cask nor its contents. My chemists were at work on their formula long before it went missing, I'm afraid, so I fear your trip here may have been for naught."

Torrum nodded solemnly. "Well then, that all seems to be in order."

Lar smiled. "I'm pleased to hear that." He rose from his seat and bowed. "Now, by all means, please do enjoy your drinks and your cigars, but I have a previous engagement that I simply must attend to. Good evening."

Svetlana watched in amusement as the Air Fleet officers, clearly at a loss for what to do, scrambled to their feet to return Lar's bow. As he walked out of the room, the officers looked at one another. Torrum finally shrugged. "I suppose we've been dismissed."

"And we trust you can find your way back to your ships," Jo said with a smile as the Air Fleet officers filed out of the room.

~

Once the Air Fleet officers were gone, Lar returned to the drawing room, where Svetlana and Jo still waited. "Well?"

"I have an important question," Jo said. "How do you get this glittery stuff off?"

"Soap, water, and scrubbing?" Lar said with a shrug. "It's meant to stay securely on during most strenuous activities."

"Wow, okay," Jo said with a playful grin. "On that note, I'm heading back to the ship."

Svetlana held up a finger. "Wait. Do you have any thoughts about what we just heard?"

"Well, I don't think Lieutenant Torrum believed a word Lar told her." Jo shrugged. "Regardless of what she said."

"You're right," Svetlana said. "Their questions seemed too easy, though. Like they knew what the answers were going to be before Lar even answered them."

Lar nodded. "It did feel that way. So did they hope that I would slip up?" He scoffed. "Surely, they know I'm no amateur."

"They would have to expect that," Svetlana mused. "None of this makes sense."

"Is there any chance that they left something, or someone, behind?" Jo asked.

Lar looked around the room. "If they left something here, we'll find it. It's unlikely that they could have left someone behind."

"That's not true," Jo said, sharing a glance with Svetlana. "Not all of the dockhands are good about taking up the slack in the strut lashings. They dangle down some. We don't think anyone got onto our ship, but someone could have used the lashings to leave their ship after the rest of them did."

With a chuckle, Lar said, "You see, Sveta? This is one of the reasons why I want you to work for me—for Rrusadon. I'll have the dockhands work on that in the future, and I'll have my security team keep their eyes open for anyone who doesn't belong."

Svetlana continued to muse over what she had seen and heard while Jo and Lar talked about the docks and searching for someone who would not want to be found. The officers the Air Fleet had sent didn't tell her anything—they had sent one person she knew, but not someone she considered a confidante or friend. Neither did their questions, their ships, or any of the other little details she often picked up give her any clues.

"Sveta?" Lar asked.

She looked up, cocking her head to the side. "What?"

"Head in the clouds?"

"Just trying to recall if there was anything we missed. But nothing. Nothing at all." She frowned. "They know something they're not telling us."

"Of course they do," Jo said, throwing her hands into the air. "The Air Fleet is all about secrets."

"I don't disagree, but I don't have an in on those secrets anymore." She paused, watching Lar closely. "There's only one person in the Fleet who might give me answers, and I'm not going to her."

"Rear Admiral March, I presume?" Lar said with a smirk.

"Yeah. But I don't think I should ask her why the Fleet showed up on your doorstep tonight." Svetlana shook her head.

"Perhaps they thought it would draw you out? Pique your curiosity?" Lar suggested.

"Hmm. Well, they're not wrong. Consider it piqued."

Lar moved toward Svetlana, smiling slyly and reaching a hand toward her bare waist. He stopped mere inches away from touching her and then glanced back at Jo.

"Right, I should be going," Jo said, chuckling softly.

"Far be it for me to drive off a charming young woman," Lar said, "but I wish you good night if you must go."

Jo winked at Svetlana. "Don't worry, Cap'n. We won't wait up for you." She slipped past Lar and Svetlana and out the door.

"Now then," Lar said softly, placing his hand on Svetlana's hip, where a wider piece of fabric draped as a very short skirt. "I couldn't help but notice that you looked uncomfortable in the clothing of one of my staff. Do you need assistance removing it, and the glitter, perhaps?" His fingers toyed with the edge of the fabric, slipping between it and her skin.

Svetlana shrugged coyly, stretching onto her tiptoes so that his hand slid farther down her hip. "I was intrigued by you saying that it's designed to stay on unless it's being scrubbed off. So perhaps we could test that theory?"

"It's hardly a theory," Lar said, placing his other hand on Svetlana's shoulder and trailing his fingers down her arm, through several swirls of gold makeup. He held up his hand, and not even a trace of the glitter appeared there.

Svetlana took his hand, lacing her fingers between his and stepping closer. She looked up at Lar, gaze locked with his. "Hmmm. I still think this requires further investigation," she said, pressing herself up against him and turning, rubbing as much of her body as she could against his shirt and trousers.

"Well, then I mustn't disagree with such an intrepid experimenter," he said, catching Svetlana mid-turn with a brushing kiss.

A knock at the door interrupted them.

Lar pulled away from Svetlana, letting out a deep breath. "What is it?" His voice was soft, but Svetlana could hear him biting back the urge to yell at whatever member of his staff had interrupted them.

"Sir, you wanted to be informed if there was any word of a ghost ship?"

Svetlana's eyes widened, and Lar looked down at her, his expression similar. "Yes?"

"Yes, sir. We've received word from Heatbourne. A ghost ship was just spotted there."

# CHAPTER FOUR

Svetlana was still painted up like one of the serving staff from Lar's house when she ran on to *The Silent Monsoon*. "Indy? How long till we can fly?"

A clatter of metal came from somewhere below decks. Hurrying down to the engine room, Svetlana found Indigo flipping switches and examining dials.

"Bad news," the boy said as he looked at Svetlana. He forced a smile but shook his head. "Two hours."

"Two hours? Why?"

"Phoebe pulled all the balloons down."

Svetlana pieced together the parts Indigo had left out. She'd requested some assistance from Lar's people to inspect the ship, since they didn't anticipate leaving quickly any time soon. Phoebe was the name of the woman he'd sent over to look at the balloons, and she'd pulled down all of the balloons to inspect the seams and ribs.

"Okay, how can we speed that up?"

Indigo shrugged. "Make the fires hotter and hope nothing tears."

"Is that safe?" Svetlana asked.

"Probably not," Indigo said. "Ask Phoebe."

"Phoebe is probably asleep, wherever she lives on Rrusadon. What do you think?"

"Probably not," Indigo repeated.

"Well, thank the Skyfather we didn't need to make a getaway earlier, eh?" she asked, patting Indigo on the shoulder. "Two hours will have to do. I'll make sure everything else is ready."

On the bridge crew hallway, all the doors were near enough together that Svetlana could stand in the center, fists out to knock, and hit all of the doors on a single spin. It was close quarters, but enough space that they each had their own room.

Athos called out, "With you in a jiff!"

Annette opened her door a moment later. "Wow, that gold stuff does stay on."

"Yeah." Svetlana signed. "We're underway in two hours. Guess I've got time to scrub it off after all."

"Where to?" Annette asked, her brow creasing. "Jo didn't say we had an Air Fleet problem when she got back."

"Not Air Fleet, this time." Speaking loud enough for the others to hear as well, Svetlana said, "A ghost ship was spotted at Heatbourne. Might be we're too late to catch her, but at least we might get a bearing on where she's bound next."

Athos popped his head out of his room. A smudge of glittery residue and soap bubbles decorated his forehead, almost glowing on his coppery skin. "Why are we taking so long to get underway, then?"

"The inspections I ordered when we brought her in," Svetlana replied. "Didn't see any reason to hurry them until now."

"Could we borrow one of Lar's ships?" Jo called from within Athos's room. "He's got a really nice new frigate that I'd love to take out for a spin."

"I'm not borrowing one of his ships," Svetlana replied, her shoulders tensing. Lar had nice ships, it was true, but it was a point of pride that she owned *The Silent Monsoon* outright. It was hers, and the idea of flying someone else's ship was a bit like borrowing a pair of recently worn shoes—the fit was off, and nothing felt quite right.

Athos nodded. "I'll see what I can do to speed up the process." He slipped out of his room, barefoot and shirtless, damp patches spotting his trousers. "Jo's mostly cleaned up if you want some help with your sparkles."

Svetlana chuckled. "Alright, help Indy out if you can. I'll go have a bath."

~

Freshly scrubbed and en route, Svetlana kept an eye on the horizon. Though it was doubtful they'd be lucky enough to spot the ghost ship that had been seen at Heatbourne, especially since it could slip in and out of Aetherwhere, she still checked the spyglass for any wavering silver ships that they might pursue.

Until recently, Svetlana had believed that Aetherwhere was nothing more than a fairy tale, quite literally. Said to be the home of the Fairy Queen, Lady de Whittvy's house on Bonebriar had made use of the extra-dimensional space that the ghost ships also occupied.

The ghost ships were just one of many straws that the crew of *The Silent Monsoon* couldn't quite grasp. Drassilis was the other big one. They needed to know Lady de Whittvy's secrets. She was the best source of information on the location of the remaining casks, and she knew how to construct the probability engine that could unlock their secrets more quickly. But a trigger-happy young ensign had closed that avenue of inquiry, so only grasping at straws remained.

Heatbourne loomed ahead of *The Silent Monsoon* before Svetlana spotted any sign of a ghost ship. The aging platform city was covered in brightly colored tents, rather than buildings like most of the other floating cities. The engineers who had constructed the early platform engines had warned that too much weight would cause cities of any substantial size to plummet into the sea, and the founders of Heatbourne had taken that advice to heart. She'd heard rumors that the powers that be in Heatbourne even required citizens of the city to weigh in periodically, and if they tipped the scales too far, they would be required to shed either pounds or possessions to make up the difference, or risk exile.

"Don't see any Air Fleet today," Jo murmured as she slowed the ship's approach to the city, preparatory to finding an available dock.

The city was thronged with airships of every shape and size, but Jo was right—none were the gleaming ships of the Air Fleet, with their distinctive navy and red balloons and flags. Svetlana pointed at a spot between a couple of ships that had seen far better days. "There's room for us there."

Jo nodded and steered the ship toward the empty slot, while Svetlana opened up the tube that let her call down to Indigo in the engine room. "Indy, how do you feel about going for a walk on Heatbourne?"

The mechanic's reply came back as a chipper "Okay!" followed by the scramble of gangly limbs.

"You and Indy?" Jo asked, a frown creasing her brow.

"We're the lightest," Svetlana replied. "Lowest landing tax."

"I hate this city," Jo grumbled. "Taxes on landing, taxes on how much you weigh, taxes on your cargo, taxes on ... I dunno, breathing next, I'll bet. They should pay us to take some of their people on as crew, save them some precious weight."

Svetlana chuckled at Jo's diatribe. "Be careful what you wish for. We take on new crew, and you might have to give up your cabin."

"Mine? Why me?"

"Your bed sees the least use out of any bed on this ship, Josephine Dean, and you know it."

Indigo rushed onto the bridge, directly between Svetlana and Jo, so anything Jo might have retorted was lost in the flail of Indigo's limbs and wavy mass of blue hair. "Red flags," he whispered, pointing out the windscreen.

Svetlana glanced at where he was pointing. "Hold our position, Jo."

"Aye," Jo said, as Svetlana strode from the bridge onto the deck of *The Silent Monsoon*.

The man waving the red flags had the dark brown leathery skin of a man who had spent his life in the elements. Where most had a pair of legs, he wore his trousers knotted on the left side at the hip, where his leg should have been. He leaned heavily on a spindly crutch that looked as though its pieces may have once earned their keep as the legs of several different wooden chairs. Svetlana recalled what Jo had said about the preoccupation of the citizens of Heatbourne over weight, and forced herself to smile only enough to seem polite, not so much as to seem as though she was laughing at the man's past misfortune.

"Is this slip not available?" Svetlana called out.

"What's yer cargo?" the man replied.

"No cargo today. Just two of us—myself and the thin boy inside—needing some conversation with the locals."

The man shook his head. "Then ya need to be docking at the landing dock, not the loading dock."

"I see," Svetlana replied. "Sorry for the confusion. Where would we find the landing dock?"

"Topside, round the back." He squinted at her. "What's the conversation yer wanting?"

"We heard tell of an unusual ship docking here," she said. "Any truth to that rumor?"

"Maybe so," the man said, clearly eyeing Svetlana's purse, "maybe not. We do see a lot of strange ships around these parts."

"Tax on everything," she grumbled. She pulled out two pence and showed them to the man. "So?"

He nodded, and Svetlana flipped the coins to him, one at a time. Once he had them both tucked away in an unseen pocket, he said, "Can't be entirely sure what I saw, but it was something I'd never seen before. Didn't stay long. "

"Did she come in at this dock or the landing dock?"

"This'un."

"So she had cargo to drop?"

He shook his head. "Nah, but she paid the tax fer what she needed to do."

"And what was that?"

He shrugged. "That'll cost ya."

"What'll it cost to let my ship drop me and the boy here, and come back for us later?"

"Three Quin. Each."

Svetlana's eyes grew wide. "What's it cost to dock topside?" she asked, hardly wanting to hear the cost.

"More," the man said, smirking.

"Give me a moment, then." Svetlana hurried back across the deck and onto the bridge. Closing the door firmly behind her, she said, "Extortionists. Remind me that if we ever get rich, we need to buy our own platform and tax everything coming and going. I need six Quinpence to get me and Indy on platform, and you'll have to circle the ship till we're through."

Jo scoffed when Svetlana mentioned the price. "Are you sure we need boots on the ground, Cap'n?"

"A ghost ship was here. I think it left something behind. I want to know what. And I'd rather go find it myself than play 'Questions for Quin' with this lout."

"You've got the purse," Jo said with a shrug.

"You think I was going to a city where they tax your weight with all my cash? Grab the box under the wheel."

Indigo reached below the direction control wheel and brought Svetlana a small wooden box, clearly much heavier than its size suggested.

She pulled the lid off, counted out six of the heavy gold coins, and nodded at Indigo. "Ready?"

"What do you think they left behind?" Indigo asked as he and Svetlana made their way to the prow of the ship, which Jo had brought closer to the platform.

"Don't know, but I hope it's worth the money we're paying to find out."

~

No children selling newspaper thronged the docks at Heatbourne. Missing, too, were the hordes of shabbily dressed children that appeared on every platform city to beg for change from new arrivals. Svetlana found it unsettling, and said as much to Indigo.

The boy nodded. "Even kids weigh something."

"So they just don't have any? That seems like a quick trip to an abandoned city."

Indigo shrugged and pointed to a crowd ahead. "Maybe ask some of them?"

A strident voice stood out from the crowd, so Svetlana approached, trying to keep Indigo within in the line of sight of her good eye. As they drew near, she understood why the young woman was shouting. A customary crier's cap holding down a mass of curly black hair, the chestnut-skinned woman read the news aloud to the assembled audience.

Svetlana scanned the crowd as she listened to the young woman. Nearly everyone wore lightweight clothing, with a narrow scarf covering their heads and necks. Heatbourne was situated in a warmer climate than Heliopolis, but the altitude of the platform cities usually rendered them cooler than they would be if they were on a landform with similar coordinates. But the weight taxes here meant that even fashion required sacrifice of warm layers and a preference for practicality. Though it made her stand out as a visitor, Svetlana was glad she hadn't shucked her coat in an attempt to bring less weight on platform. At the same time, she wondered how Indigo fared in his light shirt and pants that seemed to grow shorter with each passing day, to the point where most of his shins now showed. The boy hadn't even bothered with boots.

Without a mention of a ghost ship, the young woman reading the news was done, and the crowd began to disperse. Svetlana signaled Indigo to wait as she approached the reader. Handing the woman a small coin, Svetlana asked, "Any news of the ghost ship sighting?"

The woman looked at the coin, then smiled at Svetlana. "Thank you kindly, ma'am, but I've read all the news I know."

"Not even any stories?"

"Rumors aren't my trade."

Seizing on that, Svetlana asked, "Is there someone who does have rumors as their trade who you could direct me to?"

"Perhaps some of the shopkeepers, but I can tell you true, I've not heard a peep about a ghost ship. They're the stuff of tall tales, if you ask me."

Nodding, Svetlana said, "Well, we're something of tall tale aficionados these days." She paused. "I haven't got a place I could ask you to go if you did hear anything, but if you send a message to this blue-haired boy, it'll reach me while I'm on platform."

The woman nodded. "If I hear anything."

Now that the crowd had dispersed, Svetlana and Indigo found themselves near a market square that had been obscured before. It was quiet, with no vendors crowing about their wares like they did in Heliopolis, but Svetlana caught her first glimpse of another staple of markets all around the world—urchins.

"Know any of them?" she asked Indigo with a nudge.

He frowned in response. "Never been here before. How would I know them?"

"Secret urchin network?" she suggested.

The urchins, six of them, clustered together away from the market carts, but their gazes returned time and again to what looked like an unattended fruit stand. One of the urchins was ejected from the group and took tentative steps toward the cart. The screech of a hawk, perched atop the cart, drove the child back toward their friends.

Svetlana smiled and dug through her purse, noting the signs for the price of the fruit. Pulling out a handful of small coins, she held them in her open palm and made eye contact with the hawk. It regarded her with glittering eyes and then began preening its wing feathers. She stepped forward, still watching the bird. The sickly sweet aroma of overripe fruit hung in the air, though everything atop the cart looked unspoiled. Spotting a bowl containing similar small coins, she emptied her hand into it, and selected fruit from the cart, one piece for each urchin, plus two for Indigo and herself. As she picked up the eighth piece, the hawk squawked softly, and Svetlana nodded.

"One more?" one of the urchins asked as Svetlana handed out the fruit.

"I haven't got any more. What do you need an extra for?"

"We're taking care of a sick girl," another urchin replied, this one clearly a girl, taller and older than the rest.

"She can have mine, then," Svetlana said, handing over her piece of fruit. "Can I ask you some questions?"

The girl nodded as she bit into her fruit, tucking the extra piece beneath her arm. Faintly rust-colored juice ran down her pale chin in streams. Its tartly sweet scent wafted toward Svetlana's nostrils, and she was glad that she wasn't truly hungry at the moment. "What do they call you?"

"Beanstalk."

Svetlana forced herself not to laugh at the apt nickname, but smiled. "You can call me Svetlana. Or Captain if you like. We heard there was a ghost ship that stopped here last night?"

Beanstalk nodded, chewing a mouthful of fruit.

"Did you see it?"

The girl shook her head. "No, but we heard about it. What do you want to know?"

"We were told that something—maybe someone—got off of the ship." Svetlana looked at Beanstalk with her good eye, gauging the girl's expression. "We're looking for whatever that was."

"Someone," Beanstalk said with a quick nod. "It's the sick girl we're taking care of now."

Svetlana shared a look with Indigo. "What color is the girl's hair?"

"Dirty?" Beanstalk shrugged. "Yellow, maybe."

Indigo breathed in sharply, and Svetlana placed a hand on his bony shoulder. "Did she tell you her name?"

"Deliah."

~

The girl the urchins were caring for was none other than Indigo's friend from Heliopolis, whom the crew had not seen since shortly after departing Bonebriar. Their paths had taken them anywhere but Heliopolis, while Deliah still called that place home—or so the crew had believed. Somehow, though, she had wound up on a ghost ship, and she looked much the worse for wear.

It had taken a handful of Quinpence, along with Indigo's word that Deliah was his best friend from Heliopolis, before the urchins released their charge to Svetlana. Now Svetlana carried her back to *The Silent Monsoon*, Indigo trailing alongside and stroking the girl's hair. She weighed next to nothing. Svetlana didn't know whether that was normal or not, but she looked pale and thin, her normally bright sunshine-colored hair dull and lifeless.

The port master pursed his lips on seeing the child, his eyes narrowed. "Found what you were looking for, then?"

"Just a lost lamb who needs to see a doctor," Svetlana said. "My ship's going to need to get a bit closer this time. She can't jump across the space like we did."

The man's face was as easy to read as a book. His gaze flickered upward as though he were doing sums in the air there.

"We're doing you a favor, lessening the weight on the platform. She's already been paid for to visit." She fixed him with a hard stare, wishing she could adjust her monocular to make her blind right eye appear larger and menacing.

"Very well," he said, picking up a green flag and signaling to *The Silent Monsoon* as it approached.

By the time Svetlana's ship was in position, Annette was at the prow of the ship, concern etched across her features. "Tell me she's alive, at least."

"Just sick, according to the urchins who found her. She's light as a pillow."

Annette pulled one of Deliah's eyes open, felt at the girl's wrist, and then stretched her arms out to accept Svetlana's cargo. "She's probably dehydrated and malnourished. We'll get her fixed up in no time. She's what the ghost ship left behind?"

Svetlana nodded as she helped Indigo board the ship. "Just don't know why she would have signed on with them." She frowned. "Nor how they kept her on as crew."

"It'll have to wait until she's awake, Captain," Annette said with a shake of her head. "She won't be telling you anything until she's got a full belly."

# CHAPTER FIVE

Jo maneuvered *The Silent Monsoon* into its docking slip on Rrusadon a few hours later. "Home again, home again," she murmured. "How's the kid?"

Annette shrugged. "She's recuperating. Indy's feeding her broth now. She should be back to normal soon."

"Can we talk to her?" Svetlana asked. "Find out why she was on that ghost ship in the first place?"

"You're welcome to try," Annette said. "She hasn't said a word to me, but she also doesn't know me all that well."

Athos stood and straightened his shirt. "This sounds like a job for me."

Svetlana arched her eyebrow. "Later, maybe. She doesn't know you either, and I think she's a bit too young for your charms to work on her. If she'll talk to anyone other than Indy, it's probably me. See if you can get us a good deal on some extra food, since it looks like we're going to have a couple of teenagers on board now."

"I'll go with Athos," Annette said. "Someone's got to make sure he doesn't buy the kids a whole boatload of sweets."

"Better you than me," Jo said. "I'll see if there's anything else we need to resupply."

Svetlana nodded and headed for the infirmary. Halfway down the stairs, she was greeted with a burst of laughter and nearly unintelligible chatter.

When she poked her head through the open doorway, Indigo had squeezed onto the narrow cot beside Deliah and was making propeller sounds as he brought a spoonful of broth to the girl's mouth. She opened her mouth, bit down on the spoon, and pulled it from Indigo's hand, giggling after she swallowed. A bit of color had returned to the girl's cheeks, and her freshly washed bright orange hair clung damply to her forehead and neck.

"Glad to see you feeling better, Deliah," Svetlana said.

"Thank you, Captain." Deliah handed the spoon back to Indigo. "Are we at Heliopolis?"

"No, Rrusadon. That's where we've—" Svetlana hesitated. Deliah had proven herself trustworthy, but Svetlana had no idea who else the girl might report to. "We've stopped for now."

"I want to go home," Deliah said, her gaze avoiding Svetlana's.

Svetlana shook her head. "We can't take you there right now, Deliah. We're wanted by the Air Fleet. It's not safe for us, and it might not be safe for you, either."

"Crow Man will protect me."

Svetlana chuckled at the thought of the Crow Man, the alter ego of Lord Corwin, a prominent member of the nobility. As the Crow Man, he claimed the loyalty of a wide-ranging group of urchins, and an offer of his protection was worth a considerable amount in that group.

"I'm not sure he can keep you safe from the Air Fleet. Not without putting himself at risk, at least, and he doesn't seem like the sort to go out on a ledge for someone he doesn't consider one of his children. Maybe not even then."

"I'm not his children," Deliah said, frowning.

"No, you're not, and that's okay. You're welcome to fly with us for a while. I'm sure that Indy would be happy for the company, and we'll find you some chores to do around the ship." Svetlana paused and considered the girl. "We can take you on as a full member of the crew, if that's what you'd like."

"No. I want to go home."

"Then we'll get you back to Heliopolis when it's safe. For now, you can come with us on the ship, or you can stay on Rrusadon until we're ready to go back to Heliopolis. But I've got some questions for you, if you're feeling better."

"I need air," Deliah said suddenly and clambered off the cot. Not even pausing to put on her boots, she pushed past Svetlana, who didn't try to stop the girl. The sound of Deliah's bare feet slapping up the wooden steps in rapid succession followed.

Svetlana looked at Indigo. "What did I say?"

"Don't know. She wants to go home."

"You understand why she can't, don't you?"

Indigo nodded. "Air Fleet will lock her up because she's my friend."

"Cap'n?" Jo called down from the bridge. "Deliah just left."

Svetlana gestured toward the steps, and Indigo climbed off the cot, picking up Deliah's abandoned boots.

"I'll go find her?" he asked. "By myself?"

Svetlana considered the question. She didn't like the idea of Indigo going off alone, but she also suspected that if Deliah spotted any of the adults from *The Silent Monsoon*, she'd make herself much harder to find, and Indigo was unlikely to get too lost on Rrusadon, since he'd wandered most of the platform in recent weeks, and few other inhabitants had hair like his.

She nodded and checked her watch. "Lift is in three hours. Be back here by then, whether or not you've found her. Got it?"

Indigo knotted the laces of Deliah's boots together and slung them over his shoulder. "Aye, aye, Captain."

~

Svetlana and Jo were sitting on deck, both enjoying the late afternoon warmth. Jo had pulled off her normal blouse, wearing only a thin sleeveless shirt to expose her arms and midriff to the sunlight. Svetlana, on the other hand, leaned back in her chair, hat covering her face, but even the smallest noise made her jump. She heard Athos and Annette walking toward the ship before they'd set foot on *The Silent Monsoon*.

"Look at this," Annette said with a chuckle. "We've been out working, and they're sunbathing." She nudged Jo's leg with the toe of her boot. "Scoot over, lazybones. I want to soak up some of this sun too."

"It's not as though we're vacationing here," Svetlana said, rising from her seat. "Plenty of food?"

"Some of it's being delivered in the morning, but yes, we've got enough to keep us for a few days," Athos said. "Are we planning on casting off again?"

With a shrug, Svetlana said, "I'm not sure what we're doing yet. I'd like to talk to Deliah, but she ran off. Indy's out looking for her."

"What are you hoping to get from her?" Annette asked, stretching out languorously on Svetlana's deck chair and turning her dark face up toward the sun. Her dark copper skin gleamed in the bright light, and her lips settled into a broad smile.

"Our next step," Svetlana said. "I know her clues haven't been the best, but I'm not sure where else to look. Especially not without Lady de Whittvy or Drassilis."

"We've been over the possibilities," Athos said, shrugging, and taking care to stand so that his shadow didn't fall across Jo or Annette. "No one is sure where the other casks are. I doubt Deliah's going to have that information."

"You're likely right," Svetlana said, leaning against the bulkhead and stretching, "but I can't help thinking that ghost ships are tied up in this somehow. I don't know if there's just the one that helped us at Bonebriar, or if there are more, but there are only two people I've ever met who have flown on one, and one of those people is dead. So I want to know if Deliah saw anything, or heard anything, or has any information from the ghost ship she was on."

"Good luck with that," Jo said. "That kid doesn't make sense on a good day."

"Do you have a better idea?" Svetlana asked.

"I get that we don't want the Air Fleet getting hold of the rest of the casks," Jo said, leaning forward in her chair, "but I can't help but think they've got a leg up on us. They've got how many ships? We've got one. What if we just wait until they've rounded up the remaining casks and then steal the information from them?"

Annette chuckled. Her speech slow and lazy, as though she were on the verge of falling asleep, she said, "While that sounds like the easy way, do you really think no one would notice any of us at Air Fleet Headquarters? Even if we somehow weren't wanted for questioning, we've become infamous. Plus, if I were Air Fleet? Headquarters would be the last place I'd keep that sort of information, because they know that's the first place we'd look for it."

"Well, yeah, it's Headquarters," Athos said. "Of course we'd look there first. But Annette's absolutely right. They're going to put any information they've got into a location that we wouldn't suspect. And sure, we could make a list of the least likely places, but much like they've got a lot of ships, there are also a lot of unlikely places for them to store information." He shook his head. "Have the Kavisolis gotten anywhere with the map from Vertil—can I just call her Lady de Whittvy?"

"If you insist," Svetlana said. "I'd rather think of her as a brilliant scientist than a noblewoman."

"Noble *thief*," Annette said.

"That's redundant," Jo spat back. "But Athos has a point. Can we just narrow it down from the data your scientist girlfriend had?"

Svetlana sighed. The ribbing from her crew was nothing new, but she preferred to not think about Vertiline right now. "The Kavisolis aren't getting much of anywhere with the map. They need a probability machine like Lady de Whittvy's. Maybe Drassilis knows how to rebuild it, but he's still a pile of parts right now, and I'm not sure we're ever going to get him back up and running."

"Then I think we're going to have to find some way to locate the casks," Athos said with a shrug. "No two ways about it."

"Agreed," Svetlana said. "And while we could bounce around to all of the many and various estates of the families who still have casks hidden away somewhere, that seems like a last plan, not an immediate plan. I'd rather start with the part that doesn't involve wild goose chases."

"You got nothing from your books?" Jo asked Annette.

"Only the lists we already had. There's probably ten places we could look." Annette shrugged. "Or we'll have to ask the families themselves."

"If word gets around that we're sniffing around at too many places without finding anything, then that's narrowing down the list for anyone else who's looking," Svetlana said. "I've got half a mind to ask Lar if we can borrow one of his boats, but I really don't want to sail around as a Kavisoli, either." She squinted her good eye up at the restored rose balloon near the front of *The Silent Monsoon*. "I think we may need to consider overhauling our colors."

Athos strode over and stared openly at Svetlana's face. "Have you been too long in the sun, Sveta? I can't believe the words coming out of your mouth."

Svetlana shook her head. "I know. It's not like me to give up my old black, blue, and red. But I'm thinking something much less noticeable is going to suit us better for a while. Should have thought of it when we had the balloons down for inspections. At the very least, we can drape the smaller balloons with tarps. We'll lose a little altitude and speed, but we'll be a lot less conspicuous."

Jo frowned, looking as though she wanted to disagree with Svetlana's plans, but she held her tongue.

Athos shook his head. "You're not wrong. I'll see what I can find."

"Let's wait until Indy gets back." Glancing at her watch, Svetlana continued. "It's an hour until Lift, and I told him to be back before that. Then we'll see what our options look like."

~

Indigo and Deliah scurried onto the ship moments before the bells rang for Lift. Both of the teenagers were out of breath, faces flushed.

"Come down to the mess once you can talk," Svetlana called to them from the open doorway of the bridge. She followed Annette, who had been waiting with her on the bridge, down below.

"I'm a little surprised she's running already," Annette said.

"Never underestimate the infinite energy of youth," Svetlana said wistfully. "I remember when I could go days without eating, or days without sleeping, and not feel like death warmed over."

"Oh, I've done it too," Annette said. "The not eating part is the part I don't want to ever relive."

In the mess, Athos and Jo had already moved the tea pan to the table, with mugs set out for the whole group.

"About time," Jo said.

Indigo and Deliah followed close behind Svetlana and Annette. Hurrying around the table and peeking in the mugs, Indigo found the two with huge heaps of sugar awaiting tea, and pointed Deliah to the seat beside his.

Deliah waited until the tea had been poured, and then spoke in a quiet voice. "I think they made me escape."

"They who?" Jo asked.

"The ghosts."

Svetlana sat down across from Deliah and looked into the girl's dark eyes. "What is it that the ghosts want?"

"Like you. Find the whiskey and the secrets."

"Can we get back to the part where you think they made you escape?" Athos asked, stirring his tea. "That sounds ominous."

Deliah stared at the steam coming off the top of her mug. "They unchained me and then ignored me. When I left, I think they watched." She shrugged. "I didn't like it there. They didn't have the right ghosts."

52

Svetlana frowned at that. "What are the right ghosts?"

"Not what, who. Nice ones."

"Okay, so they only have mean ghosts on their ship?"

"Mostly."

Svetlana opted not to pursue Deliah's delineation of nice and mean ghosts for the moment. "So they're looking for the casks. Have they found any of them? Do they have a map like—" Svetlana trailed off. She'd been the only one of the crew who had actually seen Lady de Whittvy's map.

"They say they've found all the whiskey," Deliah replied. "And they'll get to the treasure first, too."

"How would that work?" Jo asked. "They can't exactly find the treasure without the map, right?"

"They shouldn't be able to," Svetlana said. "I mean, that's the whole point of the casks and the map. To keep the treasure hidden."

"Who hid it?" Indigo asked.

"The Last Emperor," Annette replied. "Or at least that's what the legends say. Though it was less of him willfully hiding it and more of him going to his final resting place with all of his belongings."

"In some sort of wreck, wasn't it?" Athos asked. "Are we going to be looking for this treasure in a shipwreck? Beneath the boiling waves?"

Svetlana grimaced. "I've been holding out hope that wouldn't be the case. But you know the way my luck tends to swing."

"Bad to worse," Athos grumbled. He looked at Deliah. "Okay, any good news from the ghost ship, or is it all just awful?"

Deliah chewed at her lip, her gaze darting to Indigo.

The boy turned toward her, mug blocking most of his face. "Ouu ell em."

"ULM?" Jo asked.

Indigo set down his mug. "You tell them," he said more clearly, looking at Deliah.

"Someone knows where a cask is, and I know how to find him."

"Who?" Svetlana asked.

"Lord Mayor Silver. He wouldn't tell the ghosts anything."

"Lord Mayor Silver was kidnapped," Annette said slowly. "By a ghost ship, wasn't it?"

Deliah nodded. Her dark eyes looked haunted.

"Where is Lord Mayor Silver?" Svetlana asked.

"Orwall."

# CHAPTER SIX

Despite Indigo diverting excess heat from the boilers onto the bridge of *The Silent Monsoon*, the air was chillier than Svetlana liked. Her breath created wispy puffs in the air when she spoke. "How much farther?"

"We should be able to see Glimmeredge soon," Jo said. "Or at least we could if the windscreen wasn't frosting over again."

Athos flexed his fingers. "I'm barely thawed since the last time I cleared it. Are you sure we don't have any more layers I can put on?"

"It's not my fault that you only buy clothes in lightweight silks and linens," Svetlana said as she pulled off a pair of slim fitting leather gloves. She tossed them to Athos. "Try not to stretch them too much."

Athos wound one of Jo's scarves over his lower face and ears, then pulled on Svetlana's gloves. "Back in a flash."

A swirl of snowflakes heralded a cold blast of outside air, and Svetlana regretted giving up her gloves. A moment later, scraping sounds came from outside the bridge, and a beam of sunlight hit the snow-coated roofs of the buildings of Glimmeredge. Beyond the town, white mountains loomed, almost blinding in the wintery sunlight.

Annette stepped onto the bridge from below, carrying four steaming mugs with her. She pressed one into Jo's hands and another into Svetlana's. A third she set on the navigational charts, then covered it with a mismatched saucer and draped a thick woolen cap over the top. Finally, she took a sip from her own as she looked out the windscreen. A smile rose to her lips. "Oh, it's lovely here."

"Lovely?" Svetlana asked with a scoff. "It's cold is what it is. I'm not sure there's enough warm clothing in the whole of Glimmeredge to keep us from freezing on our way to Orwall."

"You've never spent much time in the snow, have you, Captain?"

Svetlana shook her head.

"You warm up more than you think when you're out doing physical activity. All those layers help keep your body heat working for you. We'll be fine, as long as we keep our ears, noses, fingers, and toes well covered."

"Yes, those all seem like important parts," Svetlana said. "I hate the cold because it means we're going to have to keep the boilers running around the clock if we want the balloons to stay inflated."

"Well, if it helps any, I'm happy to go along on the expedition to Orwall," Annette said.

Svetlana chuckled. The ship's doctor rarely volunteered for most of the crew's normal outings. But this was a little more in Annette's element, since Svetlana didn't anticipate much need for fighting or lying. "Noted. Jo?"

"I can come along," Jo said with a shrug. "It doesn't make sense to take Indy, which means Deliah won't go either. And Athos—" She shook her head. "He can't handle the cold."

"Alright, then that's settled. We'll land in Glimmeredge, buy what we need, and find ourselves somewhere that has a fireplace to stay the night. If we set out in the morning, we should be able to reach Orwall in a couple of hours, right?"

Annette shook her head. "'Fraid not, Captain. If there weren't snow, that might be the case, but we'll be hiking, uphill, and with snow weighing us down." She moved Athos's covered mug to the side and examined the map. "Five or six hours, if we're lucky." She paused. "We're going to have to set out at daybreak and hope we can find a place to stay in Orwall. It'll be all but abandoned at this time of year. There's too much danger of avalanches."

Svetlana shrugged. "I suppose that's why the ghost ship decided to stash the mayor there. No one else to spot him."

Athos slipped back inside, bringing with him another gust of cold air. He spied the woolen cap on the map and grinned broadly. "Hot tea, and a warm hat? You're too good to me, Doctor Campbell."

"I'm aware," Annette said. "Jo, I've got a thought. Don't head for the docks at Glimmeredge yet. Fly toward Orwall instead."

"I thought we couldn't dock at Orwall," Svetlana said.

"We can't. But I've never actually hiked in this area. I want to get a look at what we'll be encountering, in terms of the terrain."

Svetlana smiled. "Brilliant as always. Let's see what we can see."

Jo nodded and steered the ship away from its trajectory toward the docks. Dropping *The Silent Monsoon* to a lower altitude, she wrinkled her nose. "It's nothing but snow out here."

"It looks that way, yes," Annette said, staring out the window at the side of the bridge. "But there's land underneath the snow, and that's what we need to worry about." She shook her head. "It's rocky. It'll be rough going." She turned away from the windows and began jotting a list on a scrap of paper.

In the distance, the Silver estate at Orwall loomed. It looked more like a castle of the sort found in story books than any building Svetlana had ever been inside, far more substantial than those found on the platform cities. Though the roofs were covered with a heavy load of snow, all of the walls were stone, the only wood on the building in the window frames.

"Why don't they have a dock up here?" Svetlana asked.

Jo tapped one of the dials beside the horizontal controls. "Because keeping the balloons fully inflated in this cold of weather is almost impossible. Unless these mountains are full of coal, it would be a huge drain on the city's resources."

"And it's not coal they mined here," Athos said. "Just rock. Lots and lots of rock."

"Can't burn rock," Jo quipped.

"I suppose that's true," Svetlana said. "Alright, let's just fly up past the estate house, and then swing back to Glimmeredge. I really hope those ghosts weren't feeding Deliah bad information."

Jo nodded and pulled back on the horizontal controls to give the ship a bit more altitude for their fly-by of the Orwall estate. Then she shifted her attention to the vertical controls to swing *The Silent Monsoon* into a wide, arcing path that would give the crew a good view of the house from the port windows.

Svetlana adjusted her monocular, but the device did little to improve her view of the house. She leaned forward and squinted her good eye at a slender stone minaret on one end of the building. A wide band of the roof was visible, where the snow had fallen away. "Athos, take a look at that minaret and tell me if I'm seeing things?"

Athos joined Svetlana at the window. "Well, it's a minaret all right. What am I ... wait, that looks like it's had something tied to it."

"Then I'm not seeing things. Jo, can we get any closer?"

"We can fly up and kiss it if you want to go outside," Jo said. "But I suspect you might get your lips stuck to it, what with the cold."

Svetlana scanned the ground below the minaret, which clung to one end of the estate like an aeronaut in a ship's rigging. "There's a trail on the ground. It looks like something dragged a sled through the snow."

Athos turned back to Jo. "So, let's say we wanted to stop here for a bit."

Jo furrowed her brow. "We still need warm clothing and gear from Glimmeredge."

"Trust me, I know," Athos said. "But we can anchor on to something like that minaret, right?"

"Sure, that's easy, but you'd want me and Indy to stay with the ship if you lot are going to go follow that trail. I'd need him to keep the boilers cranking out steam to keep us from dropping down and impaling the ship on that thing."

Svetlana nodded. "Athos, fancy a walk in the snow?"

"Without warm clothing?"

Annette shrugged. "We've likely got enough clothing and blankets on board that we can load up three of us with layers enough to keep us warm out there."

"Maybe for you," Athos said, looking at Svetlana. "Would it matter if I declined?"

"I'm not going to force you to do it, if that's what you're asking," Svetlana said. "But I think it makes more sense to have three on the ship, three off the ship. So unless you want to shovel coal with Deliah—"

"Right, I'll come along," Athos said.

"Not back to Glimmeredge, then?" Jo asked.

Svetlana nodded. "Looks like not."

~

Svetlana, Athos, and Annette moved slowly across the wintery terrain, bundled up with more layers than they could comfortably wear. Annette had insisted upon starting out with this much clothing, assuring Svetlana and Athos that they would be able to shed a few layers as they went. She carried a large backpack for that exact purpose, while Athos and Svetlana carried provisions.

The trail was hard to see under good conditions, but Svetlana, wearing tempered glass goggles rather than her monocular, could barely tell what Annette was following. What had been apparent as sled tracks from above were far less clear on the ground, but Svetlana trusted the doctor to guide them to the right location. Both Svetlana and Athos had their pistols near at hand, despite Annette insisting that the likelihood of misfires was high in the snow.

Annette led the group into a steep area with considerably more rock. A sled lay abandoned beside the trail, and half a dozen sets of footprints continued farther up the mountainside. Pausing, Annette crouched to examine the trail. "It looks like someone was wearing skis here, but I don't know how they could have. Going uphill, in skis, on a trail that winds so frequently isn't easy. Even snowshoes wouldn't do us any good here."

"Nor does half of what I'm wearing," Athos grumbled. "Are you sure I can't take off another layer?"

"Do you like your skin to be all glowing copper, Athos?" Annette asked.

"Of course."

"Then don't take off another layer, or you'll wind up as pink as Svetlana does when we talk about Lar," Annette replied, her eyes sparkling above her scarf.

Svetlana arched an eyebrow at Annette. "Really? That's all you've got?"

"The thrill has worn off, I see," Annette said. She turned away and scanned the path ahead. "Ten people missing from Starryglass, right? Do you recall the list of who?"

"Lord Mayor Silver, wife and children, and household staff. Maybe an advisor or two," Athos said.

"Hmmm," was Annette's only response as she moved forward again.

The terrain grew more treacherous as they gained elevation, with rocky outcrops littering even the trail they followed. Annette remained sure-footed as they traversed the faint path, but Svetlana found herself teetering with each step if she didn't place her spiked boots in the exact location where Annette's feet went.

"People do this for fun?" Svetlana grumbled under her breath.

"It takes a bit of getting used to," Annette admitted. "But yes, it can be fun. When you reach the top of a place where no one else has been, the serenity is unbelievable."

"I'll take your word for it," Athos shouted.

A low rumbling sound came back from the mountain.

Annette shook her head, her gaze going to a higher portion of the peaks ahead. "Keep your voices down," she murmured. "This area might be more prone to avalanche than I thought."

"Alright," Svetlana said. "Then silence unless we need instructions."

Annette nodded, and Svetlana hoped that Athos did the same behind her, but she didn't dare look back to check.

Somewhere nearby, a cracking sound broke the stillness. Rumbling followed, and Annette looked up, then back toward Svetlana and Athos. "Move, now! If you fall, crawl!"

Svetlana struggled forward, not able to gain much speed, but at least covering some ground. Around her, snow fell in sheets, intermixed with larger clumps.

Athos grabbed Svetlana around the waist and tried to shove her farther ahead of him, but the motion knocked both of them to their knees. As Annette had instructed, Svetlana crawled, finding it easier to move with all four limbs on the ground.

The only trouble was that the heavy snowfall made it impossible to see where she was going, and she slammed her shoulder into a tall rock outcropping beside the path. Pain radiated through her limbs, increasing the pain from the cold.

Svetlana hesitated, then closed her eyes. She ran her gloved hands across the terrain, identifying the difference between the trail through the rocks and the rubble near the foot of the outcroppings. Slowly, she felt her way back to the trail and then moved forward, pausing and adjusting any time she felt many small rocks moving beneath the snow.

After several minutes, the heavy snowfall stopped and returned to the gentle snowfall that they had been hiking through. Annette stood ahead of Svetlana on the path, and Athos, still on all fours, was just behind Svetlana.

"Good job," Annette said quietly as Svetlana and Athos stood. "That wasn't bad, as avalanches go, but once there's been one, we're at a greater risk for more. Stick close." She shook her head. "We should have brought some rope to keep us all together."

"Sadly, no rope out here," Svetlana said as they continued forward.

The trail evened out as it rounded a bend, and Annette held one hand out to her side. Ahead, a thin plume of smoke emerged from a cave mouth.

Svetlana stepped to Annette's side, avoiding the rockier patches of ground as she did. "What do you suppose it is?"

"The trail goes in and doesn't come out. It's either ghosts, who I don't think leave footprints, or it might be the Lord Mayor and his entourage."

Svetlana nodded as Athos joined the two women. "So, how does one knock in a situation like this?" Svetlana murmured.

"Shouting's out of the question, I suppose," Athos replied, his voice low.

A faint glimmer came from the mouth of the cave, and Svetlana grabbed her crew members by the shoulders. "Duck!"

A projectile whizzed past the spot where Svetlana had been a moment before, and she threw her hands into the air. "Don't shoot," she called out, trying to project her voice without being too loud.

A figure stepped forward from the mouth of the cave, rifle still held in one gloved hand. The upper half of their body was swaddled in layers like the crew of *The Silent Monsoon* wore, but their lower half consisted of two slender curved wooden blades, almost like the rockers of a rocking chair.

"Not skis," Annette murmured with a slight chuckle. "Prosthetics."

"Jayapriya?" Athos said, his question tinged with amusement.

Though the figure's face was completely covered, their head tilted to one side. "Do I know you?" a woman's voice replied.

"Athos Tucker," he said, scrambling to his feet. "We met, oh, years ago. At Wavemeet."

Jayapriya stiffened and laughed bitterly. "Oh, Athos Tucker. I remember you." She leveled her rifle. "Give me a reason why I should not shoot you here and now?"

Athos paused, raising his hands. He glanced at Svetlana and shrugged.

Svetlana took advantage of Athos's silence to rise from her crouched position. "We have an airship, and can get you out of here, if you'd like."

Another laugh came from Jayapriya, this one more mirthful. "That is a good reason. Come in out of the cold, then, the lot of you."

~

Inside the cave, Svetlana, Athos, and Annette shucked off their warm weather gear. One of Lord Mayor Silver's staff tended a roaring fire that kept the interior of the cave as warm as they might have been indoors. The woody smoke scent suffused the small space, covering the aroma of whatever was cooking in the small pot hanging over the fire. In the distance, they could hear the delighted giggles of small children, but only the servant, Jayapriya, and the Lord Mayor were near the fire.

Jayapriya had removed her layers as well, and beneath them, she was a plump but muscular copper-skinned young woman, dressed in fabrics edged with glittering threads that sparkled in the firelight. Delicate golden chains attached rings on either side of her nose to her ears and draped across her forehead and black hair.

Compared to the Lord Mayor, she appeared more suited to the title than he. Lord Mayor Silver walked with a slight stoop, though he looked too young to have been afflicted with the deteriorating joints of age. His watery blue eyes peered out from beneath a brimless grey cap and a dark shock of hair that looked almost black in the firelight. His clothing was simple woolens with no decoration to speak of.

"Jaya tells me you've offered to take us home," he said, his voice strident despite his weakened appearance.

Svetlana bowed her head slightly. "I can't say for certain that we can get you to your home, but we can at least get you to a place with an airwave station. Forgive me for asking, but why aren't you at Orwall?"

Lord Mayor Silver shook his head. "The estate there is far too large to maintain with such a small number of staff. The ... well, whatever they were that took us, only took my personal staff. It was far easier for us to go into the mountains, to a place I played when I was a boy."

Jayapriya spoke up. "We do not venture to the Orwall estate in the dead of winter. When we come here in the summer, we bring our own provisions from Starryglass. We have been making do with what we could find in the estate."

"I see." Svetlana frowned. "May I ask you about the, shall we say, pirates who took you from Starryglass?"

With a snort, Jayapriya said, "They lack the courage to call themselves pirates. They feared my blades."

"As well they should," Athos said, favoring Jayapriya with a winning smile.

Jayapriya sneered at him in return.

"Very well," Svetlana said. "But what can you tell us of them?"

"They wanted to know where we keep our Cranglimmering," a woman's voice said from just outside of the light of the fire. A moment later, a tall woman, her visible skin dark chestnut brown, and draped in layers of gauzy fabrics that clung to woolens beneath, stepped into view. She held one hand in front of her as though she was searching for something, and Lord Mayor Silver hurried to her side, taking her hand and leading her to a seat beside the fire. The woman lifted the veil from her face, revealing milky white eyes in a smooth, dark brown face.

Svetlana glanced at Athos, who mouthed back, "Lady Silver."

"Lady," Svetlana murmured. "Did you offer up the location of your Cranglimmering?"

Lady Silver laughed, joy evident on her face. "Of course not. It was clear to me that they would treat us no better if we gave them an answer, so why should we share our secrets?"

Lord Mayor Silver remained at his wife's side, still clasping one of her hands between both of his. "It was Reem's suggestion that we not tell them anything. It has landed us here, but there are worse places to be."

"Do you feel you will be safe if we take you to somewhere that you can contact your people in Starryglass?" Svetlana asked.

"It will at least be warmer," Lady Silver replied. "Where is it that you plan to take us first?"

"Rrusadon, Lady. We have friends there."

"Rrusadon? I see." Lady Silver inclined her head toward Jayapriya. "Jaya?"

"There are worse places to be, as His Lordship says," Jayapriya replied. She turned her attention back to Svetlana. "Though I wonder about the sort of people who keep friends among the Kavisolis."

"I have not yet met Mayor Kavisoli," Lord Mayor Silver said.

"I can assure you that you will find him a great deal more congenial than you might expect the Kavisolis to be," Svetlana replied quickly. With a deep breath, she continued. "I do have another question for you, Lord Mayor. While I understand that the location of the Silver Cask is a deeply guarded secret, we have reason to believe that the interior of the cask contains information that we find ourselves in need of."

"The Long-Cursed Map," Lady Silver said flatly.

Svetlana glanced between Annette and Athos before returning her attention to the Lord Mayor's wife. "Long cursed?"

Lady Silver shrugged. "The so-called pirates were not so secretive about why they wanted our Cranglimmering, and that is what they called the information inside. It does not shock me to learn that there are others after it."

"I see," Svetlana said. This was the first she had heard of a curse related to the map, and though she previously hadn't believed in magic, her experiences with ghost ships had caused her to rethink her world view. As she considered this possibility, she decided that even if the map was cursed, she had reason enough to believe that it would also bring great reward, and that was enough to settle her decision on pursuing it further.

"To what does this Long-Cursed Map lead?" Lord Mayor Silver asked.

Svetlana hesitated. She didn't believe that the Lord Mayor would ask such a question if he already knew. That he didn't know, and that no one else had already rescued him, suggested that he was not colluding with the High Council or the Air Fleet. He did not seem to be an overly ambitious man, either, of the sort who might want the Gem of the Seas for his own. His wife and bodyguard, on the other hand, might not be as docile as he.

But Svetlana also doubted that the Silver family would easily give up the location of their cask and its contents, just because she and her crew were willing to rescue them, especially if they knew her real reasoning for wanting to locate it, so she opted for an accurate, though simplified, answer.

"Treasure."

Lord Mayor Silver chuckled. "Of course. What makes this treasure so special that the map to find it has been cursed? And that would cause you to venture out to Orwall to find me? I doubt you do this out of the kindness of your own heart."

Svetlana nodded. "It's a substantial treasure. Far greater than the sort we might normally find. One that has been lost for some time."

"And you believe that this Long-Cursed Map, inside our cask, will lead you to it?"

"I'm sure of it, Lord Mayor," Svetlana said, her voice soft.

"Well, if such is the case, I suppose our cask won't remain safe for long," he replied. "Better for us to retrieve it before we leave."

"Retrieve it?" Annette said, her voice shaky. "From where?"

Lord Mayor Silver smiled at Annette. "The Needle Spires."

# CHAPTER SEVEN

Jo listened to Svetlana's recounting of the Lord Mayor's tale in silence until the captain mentioned the location of the Silver Cask.

"You mean the Needle Spires that can't be flown into or out of?"

"Never say can't," Svetlana said. "It's just highly inadvisable."

"Like the abyss is a highly inadvisable location to go anywhere near," Jo retorted. "I *know* I'm one of the best damn pilots out there. So you know it's bad when *I* say they can't be flown into or out of."

"Well then get ready to show off your skills, Jo Dean, because we're going in."

"Also, 'Long-Cursed Map'? That's new information. How sure are you that we want this map?"

Svetlana grinned, arching her eyebrow. "If you were going to create a map that leads to what is possibly the greatest treasure the world has ever known, would you call your map the 'Totally Not Even a Little Bit Dangerous Map,' or make up some rumors about curses and horrible fates?"

"You may have a point there," Jo said. "Have you asked Athos and Annette how they feel about this curse?"

With a nod, Svetlana said, "They're more concerned about the location of the cask than the possibility of a curse."

"Sounds about right." Jo shook her head. "Can I just say that this whole plan reeks? Kids—little kids—underfoot, along with a Lord Mayor and his entourage? How much are we sure we can trust him?"

"Maybe we can't," Svetlana said with a shrug. "But he'd be a fool to turn on the people who are rescuing him from living in a cave in the snow. As for the kids, I don't think they'll be underfoot all that much. They've got their mother and a nanny keeping track of them." She looked out the window. "You ask me, the one you want to keep an eye on is the bodyguard."

"Oh? Why's that?"

"Because she knows—" Svetlana hesitated. Telling Jo that Athos had recognized Jayapriya from Wavemeet might not be the best way to make this run go smoothly. She didn't know whether Jo had ever been to Wavemeet or not, but in the Air Fleet, it had been notorious as a place for the cadets to escape the pressures of their training and blow off steam. For someone like Athos, that inevitably meant casual flings, which were not things Jo would want to hear about. "I think she may have a good guess as to what we're really looking for. And she may not feel the same level of gratefulness toward us that the Lord Mayor claims."

Annette's arrival on the bridge pre-empted any reply Jo might have made. "Clean bills of health for all of our passengers. Good thing we happened by here when we did, though. Some of the staff were coming perilously close to frostbite."

"Great," Svetlana said. "So where is the Lord Mayor? We need a plan for getting his cask out of the Needle Spires."

Annette grimaced, but said, "He's down in the mess, going over the ship's capabilities with Indy and Athos."

"I suppose I ought to join them, then," Svetlana said.

"Should we head for the Needle Spires now?" Jo asked, hands hovering above the control panel.

"Let's make sure we know what we're doing before we leave the best place to get supplies at the moment."

"Aye, Cap'n."

Heading down the staircase at the back of the bridge, Svetlana avoided the worst of the frigid outside air, though it still crept into every crevice of the ship. When she reached the lower hallway, she found herself looking at one of the Lord Mayor's young children, light brown skin and brilliant sky-blue eyes peering from beneath a mop of brown loose curls. Svetlana couldn't tell if the toddler was a boy or a girl, so she simply smiled and said, "Hey there, little one. Be careful where you're walking, alright?"

The child looked up at her, lower lip quivering, but turned and waddled into the mess before letting out a loud wail.

"Sorry," Svetlana called out. "I didn't think I'd have that sort of an effect on a child."

Lady Silver's hearty laughter echoed down the hallway. "Oh, you probably didn't. Abdel cries at the drop of a hat."

Svetlana entered the mess and surveyed the crowd gathered there. Indigo, Athos, and Lord Mayor Silver huddled near a copy of the ship's plans. Lady Silver held the crying child, Abdel, on her lap, soothing him by smoothing down his unruly hair. A pale young woman nursed the other of the Silver children, while Jayapriya paced along the outer wall, a narrow line of small windows allowing daylight to shine into the mess.

"So, the Needle Spires," Svetlana said, addressing herself to the men.

"Jo's willing to fly us in?" Athos asked, looking up with raised eyebrows.

"Willing may be a strong term. But she'll do it."

"The approach is difficult but not impossible," Lord Mayor Silver said.

"Tricky part is getting the barrel on the ship without spilling a drop," Indigo said, his words turning sing-song toward the end of his statement.

Svetlana arched an eyebrow. "It's still corked, isn't it?"

"Of course. But some of the rock is jagged enough that I doubt the cask would survive being battered against it." Lord Mayor Silver frowned. "You will try to preserve the cask as best as possible, will you not?"

"That's our goal," Svetlana said. "So, Indy, how would you get it onto the ship?"

"Plank, probably. And wedges." The boy picked up a scrap of paper and drew a rough sketch of an enormous barrel perched on what Svetlana guessed was the gangplank.

"That would give it a bit of a buffer," Athos said. "And we've got some wedges in the hold."

"Good." Nodding at Indigo and Athos in turn, Svetlana turned her attention to Lord Mayor Silver. "Anything else we need to know, Lord Mayor?"

"Can your gangplank be converted into a sled?" Lord Mayor Silver asked. "You'll need some way to pull the cask out of the cave."

Svetlana's gaze flickered toward Jayapriya, and the ease with which she had crossed the snow on her ski-like leg blades, much like the runners on a sled.

The bodyguard met Svetlana's gaze, challenge evident in her eyes. "What are you thinking?" Jayapriya spat out.

"The sled we used to bring your remaining food and fuel from the cave," Svetlana said. "That has better runners than anything we have on board."

With a nod, Jayapriya said, "I shall see to its deconstruction, and reconstruction, myself. We may yet have need of it here at Orwall."

"Of course." Looking at Athos and Indigo, Svetlana asked, "Any more thoughts on the matter?"

"More than a few," Athos said.

Svetlana crossed her arms over her chest. "Go ahead."

"I've got faith in Jo," Athos said. "But I don't envy anyone having to fly into the Needle Spires. So you'll have to excuse me while I spend the next couple of hours praying to the Skyfather that he blesses us with good winds for this extraction."

~

"Alright," Jo said, gaze running over the crew of *The Silent Monsoon* and Lord Mayor Silver's staff. "Cap'n's given me authority for assignments for this fool's errand we're about to embark upon. So. Indy and Deliah? Engine room. Svetlana, rigging. Annette, I'm gonna need you to play intermediary on comms between the bridge and Svetlana. Which means the roof."

Annette shrugged. "Then I'd best go suit up."

"So I'm comms on the bridge?" Athos asked.

"You are the communications officer," Jo replied.

Jayapriya raised a slim gloved hand. "Where do you want the rest of us?"

"In the hold, I suppose," Jo said.

"I am skilled at flying an airship," Jayapriya said, her words clipped and formal.

"Me too," Jo said with a smile.

Svetlana looked between Jayapriya and Jo. Though no one had told Jo about Athos knowing the Lord Mayor's bodyguard, it seemed that the two women didn't get along. But Jayapriya had a valid point. Now to get Jo to think it was her own idea.

"What about the rest of you?" Svetlana asked, turning to the rest of the Lord Mayor's household staff. "Anyone else interested in assisting?"

One of the women raised her hand. "I can help load the cask onto the sled."

A couple of other of the Lord Mayor's staff murmured their own agreement to help with that portion of the plan.

Svetlana nodded. "Good, then that will be once we're in position. Jo, are you going to want me back down here to help hold the ship in position?"

"I'll lock the horizontal," the pilot said with a shrug.

Annette shook her head, glancing sidelong at Svetlana. "The winds might be fierce enough that a lock won't hold us where you want us. Two on the controls is going to be the safest option."

"Well, I want you up in the rigging still while we're waiting, Svetlana," Jo said, frowning. "Fine, Jayapriya, you can be my backup pilot. Just keep out of my way until I need your help."

Jayapriya gave Jo a tight smile and bowed. "Quiet as a mouse."

"Alright, then let's do this," Svetlana said. "Places, everyone."

Svetlana tugged her gloves on as she approached the rigging. It was unusual that one of the crew needed to maneuver the airship's balloons by hand, but when flying into a narrow space, the ability to manipulate the balloons was invaluable. She wrapped pliable leather strips around her arms to protect them, and climbed up beneath the main balloon.

The air near the balloons was much warmer than the air surrounding the ship at the moment, though it smelled of sulfur from the water they boiled for the steam that kept the balloons inflated. Moving around in the warmth to attach the hooks and ropes that she would use to manipulate the balloons worked up a considerable sweat, but Svetlana kept her cold weather gear in place. Gusts of icy wind were not the sort of thing she wanted to contend with while she was hauling the balloons to and fro.

Below Svetlana, Annette paced on the roof of the bridge. Her skin was completely covered with cold weather gear, and she held the speaking tube from the bridge in one hand and a battered tin funnel in the other. Svetlana could hear little more than the wind rushing through the rigging, but when Annette raised the funnel to her scarf-covered mouth, her "aft balloon port" reached Svetlana's ears as clear as day.

Wrapping the rope for the aft balloon around her forearm, Svetlana pulled it toward herself and leaned toward the port side of the ship. The balloon dropped several feet and away from a precipitous spike of jagged rock on the starboard side of the ship.

*The Silent Monsoon* moved slowly amongst the Needle Spires. The thrum of the engines was intermittent, as though Indigo was turning them on and off on Jo's command. Every time the ship scraped through a narrow passage, Svetlana cringed at the sound, even though she knew her ship could take a little bit of abuse.

The hard smack of wood against rock as the engines surged was not something *The Silent Monsoon* was prepared for. The impact knocked Svetlana against the rigging, and she scrambled to stay in her position. In doing so, the rope and hook connected to the bow balloon fell out of her grasp and flopped down to the deck.

"Bow balloon down," Annette called out through her tin funnel.

Svetlana looked down at Annette and shook her head.

"Bow balloon down," Annette repeated.

"I can't," Svetlana shouted, unsure if Annette could hear her. Looking toward the bow of the ship, she saw the problem. One of the spires ahead had cracked and fallen toward another spire, creating an arch through which the ship needed to fly. If they didn't drop a bit of altitude, and fast, the rocks would shred all four of the ship's balloons.

Svetlana lunged toward a lower portion of the rigging, trying to scramble down to the deck. Her right arm caught in the ropes, arresting her downward motion.

The ship shuddered around her a moment before Jayapriya burst out of the bridge door. The Lord Mayor's bodyguard looked up into the rigging and locked her gaze with Svetlana's. With a nod, she picked up the rope attached to the bow balloon and reached toward the blades that had replaced her legs with her other hand. Then she launched herself into the lower portion of the rigging, climbing using only her arms, as her artificial legs clattered to the deck. She wrapped the bow balloon rope around her arm even as she climbed the rigging, and the balloon moved beneath the front end of the main balloon as she neared Svetlana.

"Caught, Captain Tereshchenko?"

"A bit," Svetlana admitted. She scanned the horizon, no longer able to see the rock arch ahead. "Are we clear of it?"

"I hope so," Jayapriya said. "If you can reach your free arm around my waist and hold me up, I can see about getting your other arm untangled."

Svetlana looped her arm around Jayapriya and pulled her close. The bodyguard smelled of cloves and smoke in a pleasant combination.

"And to think, I'm not even sure what your mothername is," Jayapriya murmured under her breath as she maneuvered Svetlana's arm free of the entangling ropes.

"Mothername?" Svetlana asked. "What's that?"

Jayapriya tensed in Svetlana's grasp. "Where I come from, we are known by our first names and the name of our mother. I ... my mother was unknown to me. When I entered the Lord Mayor's service, I took on the name of his wife as my second name. So I am called Jayapriya Reem, formally."

"Ah, then I suppose my mothername is Svetlana Ludmilla, though I never knew my mother either. She died in childbirth," Svetlana said softly.

Jayapriya bowed her head solemnly. "A pleasure to know the name of your mother, Captain Tereshchenko."

"If you know my mothername, I think you can call me Svetlana."

"As you say. But I fear we must not stay entangled as we are. Jo will need my assistance to keep the ship in position at the cave mouth."

"Of course," Svetlana said. She took the bow balloon rope from Jayapriya and released the bodyguard into the rigging. "Perhaps we can talk more later."

Jayapriya nodded. "I would enjoy that, Cap—Svetlana."

~

"So, what needs to be done to retrieve your map?" Lord Mayor Silver asked, standing in the hold of *The Silent Monsoon*, with one hand touching the side of his cask.

Although Svetlana had seen the cask staves in Lady de Whittvy's map room, seeing a fully assembled cask for the first time was something entirely different. Indigo's wedges had done the job of keeping the cask on its side, as it was meant to be. The head of the cask was nearly as tall as she was, and it looked about half again as long as it was tall. That they had extracted it from a cave in the Needle Spires without a scratch was truly an impressive feat.

"Best case scenario, when we get back to Rrusadon, we can drain the cask, disassemble it, and copy the map before we put it back together and refill it. Mayor Kavisoli has chemists on his staff who can advise us the best way to do so, for the integrity of the whiskey." She paused. "If you're feeling particularly gracious, I'm sure they would be ecstatic if you let them keep a small sample."

Lord Mayor Silver arched his eyebrow, but Jayapriya shook her head. "We appreciate what you've done for us, Captain Tereshchenko, but that is too much. The Lord Mayor's cask is invaluable."

"The Bartrams offered a mill when theirs was taken," Svetlana replied. "That tells me there is a price."

"There were four casks available then," Jayapriya replied. "Now there are but three. With each one opened, the value of the remaining casks increases."

Svetlana smiled at Jayapriya. "I see you take your whiskey quite seriously."

"I care nothing for the whiskey. I protect the Lord Mayor and his livelihood, which includes his wealth." Jayapriya did not return the captain's smile.

Svetlana wondered if their moment in the rigging had been less than she read into the situation. Nonetheless, she shrugged and continued. "I can guarantee that whatever happens to the cask while on Rrusadon will remain among yourselves, my crew, and Mayor Kavisoli's chemists. No one need know that the cask has even been retrieved, if that's your preference."

Jayapriya frowned, but did not offer a retort.

Lady Silver, who had been listening to the debate, spoke softly. "Jaya, I believe Captain Tereshchenko is right. I almost think we would be better off leaving the cask at Rrusadon. Who would look for it there?"

"As long as we can keep this daring rescue out of the papers, not a soul," Svetlana said.

"Then it is done," Lord Mayor Silver replied. "We uncork the cask at Rrusadon. I shall drink a glass in celebration of our rescue, and any of your crew who wish to partake may as well, Captain Tereshchenko. Mayor Kavisoli may have a glass to drink or to give to his chemists."

Svetlana smiled. "Oh, he'll be delighted, as well as conflicted. I can't wait to see what he decides to do."

"We're arriving," Jo's voice echoed through the speaking tube to the hold.

Svetlana gestured toward the door to the hold. "Might I ask one more question, before we go on platform? This one remains between only us."

Lord Mayor Silver arched an eyebrow, but nodded.

"We know that the Somerset and Gyrfalcon Casks are still unaccounted for as well. Have you any insight into their location?"

"I could not say when it comes to the Gyrfalcon Cask," Lord Mayor Silver said. "Our families have never been close. But there are rumors about the Somerset Cask. It is said that the family itself does not know the location of their own cask. It has been lost to the ages."

Svetlana frowned, her brow creasing. "Do the Somersets have any holdings outside of Merrowbarrow?"

"No, they maintain but the one home there. Since time immemorial, to my understanding."

"That is our understanding as well." Svetlana watched Jayapriya's retreating figure as the bodyguard led Lady Silver out of the hold. "I suppose, then, once we've seen you safely off to Starryglass, we'll be taking a trip to Merrowbarrow."

# CHAPTER EIGHT

The Silver household had departed on a ship back to their home estate, after Lar's men had retrieved the map staves from within the cask. Though Svetlana hadn't particularly enjoyed her glass of Cranglimmering any more than she had enjoyed the Kavisoli's synthetic Cranglimmering, Annette and Athos still had a dreamy look in their eyes as though they were still savoring the flavors. Athos had said something about it being like tongue-kissing a sweetwood fire, which didn't seem appealing in any way to Svetlana. She dared not tell them that in her opinion, the only good whiskey was the kind you drank fast as a painkiller, not the kind you sipped slowly.

"So what do we know about Merrowbarrow?" Jo asked, as the crew of *The Silent Monsoon* lounged in the mess, on their now blissfully quiet ship.

"Aside from the fact that the Somersets have been there for generations?" Annette shrugged. "Not much else. They're very insular. I don't think I know anyone who's ever visited."

"Marvel of engineering," Indigo said.

Svetlana turned her attention to the boy, who was poring over one of Annette's history books. "What's so marvelous about it, Indy?"

"It's a floating city that doesn't actually float," he said. "They carved away the ground underneath it to make it look like it was flying. But there's a bunch of rock that holds it up."

Athos looked over Indigo's shoulder at the book. "Oh, it's on a pillar of rock." He frowned. "That seems inefficient."

Annette nodded. "It is. But after the Boiling, platform cities were all the rage. If your city couldn't hover above the water, sometimes the nobles decided to make other modifications to make their city unique." She looked at Athos. "I take it you've never been there either, then?"

"Nah, too stuffy for me," Athos said with a shrug. "I've heard that everything is very formalized, down to things like the way you part your hair. It was on my list if I ever got truly bored, but I haven't made it there yet."

"So it sounds like just flying over there and asking after the cask is out of the question?" Svetlana asked.

"Do you really think that would work, even if we could just go ask?" Athos replied.

"Probably not, but it was worth a shot. I feel like we need some more information." Svetlana frowned, considering the options.

"I can double check my books," Annette said. "Indy, how do you feel about looking for some drawings or pictures of this marvel of engineering?"

"What about Drassilis?" the boy asked, gaze sliding over to the now tidied pile of robot parts in the corner of the mess.

Svetlana followed Indigo's gaze. "Alright, I'll go talk to Lar and see if he's ever been to Merrowbarrow, or knows anyone else who has, and I'll get you some extra hands to help with Drassilis, now that we're back for a bit. Athos, Jo, you mind helping the Doc with her research?"

"It'll go faster with three sets of eyes," Jo said with a shrug.

"Good. Indy, go ahead and get started with Drassilis." Svetlana looked at her pocket watch. "I'll be back in a few hours."

~

Lar embraced Svetlana tightly when she arrived at his room. "Sveta, my darling, I don't know how you continue to impress me. Thank you for ... there are too many things to thank you for. The introduction to the Lord Mayor, the Cranglimmering, the fact that he's allowing me to store his cask for him? I'm not even sure you know how much you've done for me."

Svetlana smiled. "I'm glad to have been of assistance. And not everything was for you, if I'm being honest. We needed those staves, if we're ever going to find the Last Emperor's Hoard."

"I still feel as though I got the better end of the bargain. Truly, Sveta, thank you."

"You're welcome." Svetlana smiled at Lar, running her hand through his thick hair. "I suppose this means you're in the mood to do me a favor?"

"Has there ever been a moment you doubted my willingness to help you?"

"Well, there was that time I couldn't get you out of Air Fleet custody fast enough for your liking," she replied with a smirk. Though they had forgiven each other for the misunderstanding, Svetlana still liked to bring it up to tease Lar now and then.

He bowed and kissed her hand. "What favor do you require of me now, darling?"

"Not a substantial one. I need you to send an airwave to Chickie. See if he'd like to come out for a visit. Don't mention my name, but somehow let him know that I need to see him?"

Chickie was the nickname of Lord Algernon Boughorppington the Third, one of the nobles who made Heliopolis his home. Lady de Whittvy, while still masquerading as Vertiline, had sent Svetlana to a party on his airship, the same one where Svetlana and Lar had first begun their intimate relationship. Chickie had become a good friend in the intervening time, even going so far as to accompany his airship to Bonebriar in support of the crew of *The Silent Monsoon.*

Lar favored her with a sly smile, then looked upward as he began composing aloud. "My dear Chickie. Come to Rrusadon and take in our most delightful sights, particularly the golden eye of the storm."

Svetlana grimaced. "Too on the nose, I fear."

"I thought it was preferable to describing any of your other features. Particularly the ones I don't think Lord Boughorpington has ever seen." Lar slipped an arm around Svetlana's waist and pulled her close to him. "How would you have me describe you, Sveta?"

"Hmmm. My dear Chickie. Come to Rrusadon. A dear friend of Madeline's wishes to see you."

"Madeline?" Lar asked, arching an eyebrow. "Is she half as pretty as you?"

"If you add an 'and her' to the airwave, perhaps you'll be able to see for yourself." Svetlana smiled. "I suppose it's good I'm not the jealous type."

"If you were, I would promise to only have eyes for you," Lar murmured, planting delicate kisses along Svetlana's hairline, heading quickly toward her lips.

"What fun would that be?" she asked, before letting him silence her with a kiss.

~

"Darling, what *are* you wearing?" Chickie asked as he leaned in to kiss each of Svetlana's cheeks after coming on board *The Silent Monsoon*, a day after Lar had sent his airwave.

Svetlana looked down at her typical trousers, blouse, and jacket. "Um, nothing special?"

"Well, you do wear it the best, that's for certain. Now, I came as soon as I got your airwave. What scandal are you hoping to drag me into this time?"

Svetlana smiled. "Not a scandal. Yet, at least. We need to go to Merrowbarrow."

Chickie pouted. "Oh, whatever for? That place is a bore."

"I tried to tell her that," Athos chimed in. "But the Somersets are there. Even if they have misplaced their cask."

"You're still on that old thing?" Chickie asked. "Very well. Then you'll be needing to see the Lady Mayor?"

"Yes," Svetlana said. "And we need you to coach us on the labyrinthine social nonsense of Merrowbarrow."

Chickie fished out his pocket watch, pretending to study it closely. "How much time do you have, darling?"

"Time is of the essence."

"Of course it is." Chickie planted his hands on his hips, tilting his head to one side. "Which of you will be going to meet with the Lady Mayor?"

Svetlana looked at Athos, who shrugged. "Who would you recommend?" she asked Chickie.

"Well, the two of you for certain, though we'll have to do something about your clothes."

"I thought you liked my clothes," Svetlana said.

"Darling, I said no one could wear them like you. That's not the same as approving them for a social call." He smiled and patted Svetlana's shoulder, somehow making his commentary seem a little less catty. "Not the child, there will be too many shiny things he'll want to touch. Same may go for Miss Dean."

Athos held up a finger and opened his mouth a few times before he spoke. "How did you know her last name?"

Chickie rolled his eyes. "How could I not know? I'm a keen observer of my surroundings, after all. She may think it's a secret, but I've heard the rumors, and I know better than to discount all of them." He turned his attention back to Svetlana. "Now then, does the Doctor want to go along? Or maybe you should take Lar. Hmmm. It should only be three, no matter what."

"What about you?" Svetlana asked.

"Me?" Chickie placed a slender hand on his chest and smiled. "Why Svetlana, darling, how kind of you. Yes, of course. That makes the best sense. I can stomp on your toes if either of you starts in a direction I don't like."

"Lovely," Svetlana said, crossing her arms over her chest. "You're not going to put me in heels, are you?"

Chickie looked her up and down, then shook his head. "No, it's not necessary. But you will need a dress. If you still have that lovely blue one from my party, I promise I won't tell Lady Mayor Somerset that you've worn it before."

Svetlana shuddered at the thought of being strapped into two corsets again, but Athos butted in before she could respond further. "We have it. How do you want to play this, though? She's your arm candy, and I'm your ... valet or something? Or do I get to be the arm candy?" Athos winked at Chickie.

Chickie tapped a finger gently on Athos's cheek. "How attached are you to your goatee?"

Athos bristled, and Svetlana took the opportunity to laugh at her friend. "Oh, come on, Athos. It's only hair. It'll grow back." She dropped her voice lower and leaned toward him. "And if I have to suffer, then so do you."

"Oh, come now, darlings. Let's not think of it as suffering. Let's call it enrichment. Learning new things! Like the way the brisk wind on an airship feels against a naked chin." Chickie thrust his chin forward, turning so that his face was in profile, showing off his well-formed features.

"You're not making this better, Chickie," Athos grumbled.

Jo poked her head out of the bridge. "Cap'n, we're refueled. How long till you want to leave?" Spotting Chickie, she gave him a flirtatious wave. "Oh, are we taking his ship instead?"

"What happened to you preferring to fly this one?" Athos asked.

With a shrug, Jo said, "I figure I should broaden my horizons."

"That is what I'm talking about, darlings. There's so much out there for you to experience. Like corsets and scones and not getting crumbs in your beard!"

"There's only one of those things I'm particularly interested in," Jo said, brow furrowing. "Where can we get scones?"

"Seems like the bar for entry to scones is wearing a corset or shaving off a goatee," Svetlana said, heading toward the forward staircase. "You, Annette, and the kids don't need to do anything of the sort. Chickie will take Athos and me into the belly of the beast."

"Alright," Jo said. "That part suits me just fine. But if you happened to drop a scone into your handbag?"

Svetlana's only response was a steely glare.

~

"I have a theory about why upper-class women don't wear their outfits more than once, Chickie," Svetlana said as she, Athos, and Chickie made their way across Merrowbarrow, dodging the brackish puddles that speckled the streets.

"Oh, why is that, darling?"

"Because it only takes wearing something once to figure out how much you hate it, and how much you never again want to suffer the pain and indignity of that particular dress. Have I mentioned that I hate corsets?"

"A few times," Athos said. While Svetlana was regretting everything about having to wear Lady de Whittvy's blue dress with the peacock accessories again, Athos looked magnificent in a starched collared shirt, snug fitting trousers, and a jacket he had borrowed from one of the Kavisolis, since nothing Chickie owned would fit Athos's broad shoulders. In the end, Chickie had agreed that unless Athos was to stand in as his arm candy, he simply needed to trim his goatee into a more fashionable shape.

Athos looked even more formal than the actual member of the nobility among them. Chickie's jacket of choice was a brilliant emerald smoking jacket in a much more relaxed cut than the one Athos wore. It made his already pale skin pop out all the more and complimented his ginger hair. He also wore it like he was born to it, which, upon consideration, Svetlana realized that he really was.

"Tell me again why they don't use carriages here?" Athos grumbled.

"Because with rainfall comes puddles, and with puddles and carriages together come horrible splashes." Chickie gestured to a wooden plank that spanned a particularly large puddle. "Careful now, darling. Lift your skirt in the front."

Svetlana did as he said, but made an unpleasant face while doing so.

"Now then," Chickie continued. "How do you propose that we approach the sensitive matter of asking after Lady Mayor Somerset's misplaced cask?"

"Because just asking is out of the question?" Svetlana asked.

"Yes, of course. We must approach such matters delicately," Chickie said. "My dear Svetlana, perhaps you should allow me to do all of the talking?"

Svetlana shook her head. "No, Chickie, you've already done so much for us. If there are rude questions that need to be asked, let me do that. I don't want to tarnish your reputation, after all."

"Too kind, darling. I do plenty of tarnishing on my own, to be honest. But very well. I shall get us through her front door, and then I leave the line of questioning to you."

The Somerset estate loomed ahead of the trio. If the platform carved from a mountain looked precarious, the house itself appeared even more gravity-defiant than the city it called home. Various wings of the house grew from the central portion like untamed weeds, some larger at higher levels than the points at which they attached to the house proper. While everything was covered with slate shingles, the amounts of foliage that grew along the edges of the shingles indicated their relative age. The broad awning across the front door showed no slate at all, but looked as though it had been thatched in green moss.

"Charming," Athos said softly. "Tell me she doesn't reside in one of those spindly parts?"

"I couldn't say for certain," Chickie replied. "I, for one, would like to take the fact that they are still attached to mean that their architects knew what they were doing."

"So perhaps I shouldn't bring up that pile that looks like a collapsed room or six?" Svetlana asked, gesturing to one side of the house where a large pile of shattered shingles was strewn across the yard. Their color was patchy slate and green with small purple and white blossoms growing between them, and everything covered with a thick sheen of the misty rain that more hung in the air around them than fell to the ground.

"Charming, indeed," Chickie said as he strode toward the front door.

Before he could knock, the door flew open, revealing a wizened old woman dressed all in black who glared at him with dark eyes.

Chickie did not falter. He bowed low and said, "Lord Algernon Boughorppington the Third, and my associates, here to call upon Lady Mayor Somerset."

"Is she expecting you?" the woman asked, her voice exactly as creaky as Svetlana had expected it to be.

"Alas, she is not." Chickie produced a calling card. "Please beg her forgiveness for our unheralded arrival."

The woman stared at the card for a long moment, then took it from Chickie's hand with gnarled fingers. She brought it within inches of her eyes and peered hard at it. "Lord—" she began.

"Algernon Boughorppington the Third," Chickie repeated. "You may tell her that Chickie is here, but I fear she will not be familiar with that name."

The old woman chuckled drily. "I see. I'll tell her you're here." She glanced past Chickie toward Svetlana and Athos. "I suppose I should have you step inside, what with the rain."

"Many thanks," Svetlana said, lifting her skirt and following the woman inside. Chickie and Athos followed her into the warm— and somewhat drier—entryway.

The inside of the house was considerably less green than the outside, but it seemed that the damp was pervasive even indoors. Here, it smelled only damp and musty, rather than outright wet and decaying.

"How does anyone live in this kind of place?" Athos murmured. "So dark and wet."

"It takes a special sort," Chickie replied, his voice also quiet.

The door that the elderly woman had disappeared through opened again, and a different woman stood there. Though her skin was wrinkled and her hair a mix of slate and silver, she had the bearing of a younger person, and stared at Svetlana, Athos, and Chickie with gray-blue eyes. "Lord Algernon Boughorppington the Third," she said. "And associates. Do I know you?"

"You do not, Lady Mayor," Chickie said with another formal bow. My associates and I hoped we might gain audience with you to ask about a bit of your, shall we call it 'family history'?"

Lady Mayor Somerset stiffened, but said, "Very well, follow me."

"You didn't happen to ask Annette if she knew anything about the Somersets before we came here, did you?" Athos whispered to Svetlana as they followed the Lady Mayor through dimly lit hallways.

"She told me what she knew," Svetlana replied quietly. "They're very insular. There's not much to know about them."

"Well, then maybe we'll come out of this with something that Annette doesn't have in one of her books," Athos said. "Won't that be something?"

"You've been spending too much time with Chickie, Athos."

"Oh?"

"You're enjoying this far too much."

"You're right. I should start grumbling about everything like Jo does."

Svetlana shook her head. "Just ... keep your eyes and ears open. I find it hard to believe that a family could just misplace something the size of a cask."

"Cask?" Lady Mayor Somerset said as she led them into a sitting room. "You're here about that old thing?"

Svetlana glanced at Chickie, then back at Athos. They had been speaking quietly enough, she thought, that their hostess could not possibly have heard them. And yet, she knew what they spoke of. "Yes, Lady Mayor. We heard that it is long lost, but wanted to inquire after it in person."

"Alas, my dear Madam, the cask was lost the day we took possession of it."

# CHAPTER NINE

———————

Lady Mayor Somerset gestured for Svetlana, Athos, and Chickie to sit in the overstuffed chairs of the sitting room. It too had a musty aroma that lingered in spite of the gas lamps on the walls, exacerbated when they all sat and stirred up whatever organisms lurked within the fabric. The mold and mildew of Merrowbarrow seemed to pervade every corner of the city, even an otherwise well-appointed sitting room.

Once her guests were settled, Lady Mayor Somerset spoke again. "Thirty-five years ago, an exquisite batch of Cranglimmering—the first since the Boiling, in fact—was placed in seven casks, and the casks were given to seven families who had been instrumental in its re-creation. I don't know what role the Somersets played, as I was young and cared little for the business of my family. I believed that my father had a long life ahead of him, and that I would marry and perhaps allow my husband my family's seat in the Senate." She shook her head ruefully. "As I said, I was young. And overly romantic. I had no ambition other than to be a wife and a mother, so long as it allowed me pretty dresses.

"But this is not the story you have come to hear. My father, Aonghas, was the eldest Somerset, and had two younger brothers, Keelan and Edwyn. The cask was presented to the Somerset family as a whole, so my Uncle Edwyn had argued, prior to our receipt of the cask, that it belonged to them all, not just my father. So they decided, the three of them, that they would hide the cask away somewhere safe. I don't know for certain, but I suspect Uncle Edwyn had something to do with that decision as well.

"So the three of them had the cask loaded onto a wagon and drove off together. That was the last time I saw my father. Only Uncle Edwyn returned, and he—" She trailed off, staring at her wrinkled hands. "He had killed Father and Uncle Keelan. He bragged of it, in fact. He said he would now be the Lord Mayor, as the surviving brother. But the rest of the family—my mother and Aunt Brigid in particular, who had both just lost their husbands—refused. They took Uncle Edwyn to the magistrates, and since he had confessed to his crimes and showed no remorse, he was tried as a formality and sentenced to death. I don't think that he expected such a harsh punishment, but he received the same sentence that any murderer would have received. The magistrates did not go easy on him simply because he belonged to the nobility. Still, he would not tell anyone where he and his brothers had hidden the cask. We thought he might have sold it, but if he did, he hid the money as well as he hid the cask."

Silence reigned when Lady Mayor Somerset finished her story. Glancing at Chickie, Svetlana asked, "May we ask you a few questions, Lady Mayor?"

Lady Mayor Somerset smiled, her eyes watery. "Of course."

"Has anyone else inquired after your cask recently?"

"You mean the ghosts?"

Svetlana gasped. "Ghosts?"

"They might appear as men and women, but they must be ghosts, because they said they came here to speak with Uncle Edwyn."

"And were they able to speak with him?" Svetlana asked.

Lady Mayor Somerset's tight smile gained a bit of warmth. "Indeed, but even in death, he refuses to reveal the location of the cask."

"How exactly did they speak with him? Were you privy to the conversation?" Svetlana had many more questions she wanted to ask about the ghosts, but she suspected she was already far overstepping the bounds of propriety.

"The ghosts made their presence known to me as any living person would—they came to my front door. But the conversation they had with my uncle seemed rather one-sided to me. I could not hear his words, but their reactions told me that the cask remains lost." She exhaled softly. "Perhaps it is better off lost. That is, you all are pleasant enough, but I have had more visitors this past week than I have had in the past thirty-five years."

"Were there more than the ghosts and us?" Athos asked.

The Lady Mayor nodded. "I have a question for you as well. What is this cask to you?"

Svetlana measured her words carefully. "We believe that the cask contains information that we seek."

"Then I suppose that explains why the High Council wants it. They can't bear to not be the ones with all of the juicy tidbits."

"Who did they send?" Chickie asked, his voice low and quiet, not at all like his usual affectations of speech.

Lady Mayor Somerset considered Chickie for a long moment before she answered. "Swaisbrook."

Chickie shot a glance at Svetlana, whose eyebrows had already shot up. "Not good, I take it?" he murmured.

"His name does seem to be in the thick of things," Svetlana replied.

"He proposed a marriage alliance between one of my great-nieces and his son," Lady Mayor Somerset said. "I have no intentions of marrying my family members for political expedience unless they themselves ask for it. The young and foolish girl I once was learned much when she was thrust into power by the death of her father."

"Then I suppose it would surprise you little to learn that High Councilor Swaisbrook had offered the hand of his son in marriage to the eligible descendant of another family who had a cask in their possession," Svetlana said.

Chickie gasped. "What? Hortence? No. Swaisbrook is completely out of touch." Then he chuckled. "My apologies, Lady Mayor. I do delight in keeping atop all the goings on of high society."

Lady Mayor Somerset nodded. "I appreciate your kind visit, but I am afraid I cannot be of more assistance to you with whatever information it is you seek. We have searched every bit of Merrowbarrow for the cask, using every method at our disposal. But we have come up empty handed."

~

When the group arrived at *The Silent Monsoon*, Indigo met them on deck, his x-ray goggles slung around his neck. "Hey, Captain. Can we go see the rock pillar now?"

Svetlana shrugged. "I suppose so. Nothing else to find here."

Indigo ran back onto the bridge.

"Oh, Captain," Chickie said. "You promise we'll be out of this poorly ventilated spa soon?"

"Yeah, we'll just do a quick fly-by to see the rock pillar. Marvel of modern engineering, and all that. At least according to Annette's history books."

As Athos, Svetlana, and Chickie stepped onto the bridge, Jo asked, "Cap'n, can I get you on the horizontal?"

"Sure. Do you anticipate trouble flying below the city?" Svetlana asked.

Jo shook her head. "Not really, but I figure we can get a good look at the rock if we can get real close to it."

*The Silent Monsoon* took off and arced out from the city of Merrowbarrow, giving them a wide view of the decaying buildings and the weathered rock beneath them. Even as they flew at this altitude, the crew saw small chunks of rock falling from various points on the underside of the city. As their path took them lower, there were places that looked like entire boulders had collapsed away from the former mountain.

A sharp inhale preceded Chickie asking, "Is that even structurally sound?"

"I don't see how it can be for much longer," Annette murmured.

"You can bring it up with the Lady Mayor, Chickie," Svetlana said. "Write her a nice letter. 'Dear Lady Mayor Somerset, we had such a lovely visit. Also, your city is collapsing from below.'" A flash of dull red caught Svetlana's eye before she could finish composing her fake letter. "Hang on, what's that?"

Athos and Annette moved to the starboard window, blocking Svetlana's view of whatever it was she had seen.

"Looks like brick, maybe," Annette said.

"Chickie, hold this position," Svetlana said.

"Me? Alright."

Svetlana relinquished the wheel to Chickie and stood between her first mate and ship's doctor. "Yeah, that. It's brick alright. Indy? Let me see your goggles."

Indigo nudged between Svetlana and Annette, the goggles casting their eerie blue glow across his pale face. "It's a really long brick box."

"Really long?" Athos asked, reaching over Svetlana's shoulder and snagging Indigo's goggles. Pulling them on, he adjusted a few of the lenses. "Yeah, I guess you could call that a really long brick box. If it were narrower, I'd think it might be a well, actually—" He paused. "Jo, Chickie, can we go lower? Maybe 50 feet?"

"Yeah, I don't see why not," Jo said. A moment later, *The Silent Monsoon* flew lower, still in a wide arc around the rock pillar that kept Merrowbarrow aloft. The setting sun pierced the clouds at this elevation, bathing everything in golden light.

"It's the Somerset Cask," Athos said, his voice trembling. "They put their cask at the bottom of a very deep cellar."

"Are you sure?" Svetlana asked. "Gimme the goggles."

Athos slipped them off and grinned. "It's almost full, too."

Donning the goggles, Svetlana took a bit longer to adjust them than Athos had. They had no magnification capabilities like her monocular did, which meant that she couldn't even see a blur on her right-hand side. Getting the lenses to focus enough to compensate for her blind eye was challenging. Suddenly, she had it right, and the details etched in blue swam into detail.

Crumbling bricks peeking from within the rock surrounded a large wooden cask. And as Athos had said, the cask was nearly full, with only a small gap between the whiskey and the top of the cask.

"Any chance that the damp has gotten into it and refilled it?" Svetlana asked.

"It's not likely," Annette replied. "Casks are meant to keep the elements out and the contents inside. They lose a bit to evaporation, but the casks that the coopers make for the long-aging whiskeys are pretty solid. Can I see?"

Svetlana passed the goggles on to Annette, who nodded as soon as she had them adjusted. "Yeah, that's gotta be it." She craned her neck, looking toward the higher portions of the pillar. "I can't see it all from here, but it looks like someone might have a very deep, unused basement, and that's where the Somerset Cask has been hidden all this time."

"Wouldn't you think the Somerset family would have checked there?" Jo asked. "I mean, we can't be sure this is *the* cask, exactly. Not without seeing it."

Svetlana nodded. "That's probably true. But, at the same time, can anyone else think of any other extra-large whiskey casks of note that are supposed to be in Merrowbarrow?"

Most of the crew shrugged, but Annette shook her head firmly. "There aren't any other whiskeys that I can think of that were barreled in anything even close to the same size as the Cranglimmering. There are shelves of treatises on whether that was a good or bad thing, in terms of the production and storage of whiskeys."

"Doc, you being a whiskey historian is probably my favorite thing about you," Athos said. "Well, that and patching us up when we get in trouble."

"Thanks, I think," Annette replied.

Turning back to Svetlana, Athos asked, "So, Cap? How in the abyss are we going to get a full cask of whiskey out of an unstable landmass?"

"Cart before the horse," Svetlana said, shaking her head as she removed the goggles and replaced them with her monocular. "First we've got to convince the Lady Mayor to let us move her cask."

~

"Back so soon?" Lady Mayor Somerset asked as she regarded her guests. Svetlana and Chickie had returned to the Lady Mayor's house, with Annette in tow this time. For her part, Annette was doing a remarkable job of not panicking over the deteriorated state of the house surrounding them.

"We thought you should be the first to know that we may have relocated the Somerset Cask," Svetlana said.

"Where did Uncle Edwyn hide it?" Lady Mayor Somerset asked, her eyes sparkling with a mixture of excitement and anger.

Svetlana glanced at Annette. "If our mapping is accurate, in an unknown portion of what was once his family's home."

The Lady Mayor frowned. "Then how—"

"Lady Mayor, the landmass that holds Merrowbarrow aloft is deteriorating," Annette said. "I'm no engineer, but the city appears to be approaching a level of instability that your builders may have a difficult time compensating for. There are chunks of the mountain below that have fallen away from the pillar the Somersets carved all those years ago. If just a few more chunks fall away, they'll expose your uncle's basement, which extends several stories beneath the surface of Merrowbarrow."

"My uncle's estate was not far from the center of Merrowbarrow at one point. If his basement is imperiled, then you are quite right. I suppose we cannot ignore the danger much longer." Lady Mayor Somerset shared a wry grin with her guests. "And I had hoped we would retrieve the cask before we were forced to move elsewhere."

"Lady Mayor, none of my crew are engineers, but we're almost certain that the cask cannot be removed from the basement without destabilizing the rock around it substantially." Svetlana paused, gauging the expression on the Lady Mayor's face. So far, she was listening with rapt attention, with her brow only faintly furrowed. "We'd like to propose an alternate means of removing your Cranglimmering from where your Uncle Edwyn left it."

Lady Mayor Somerset arched an eyebrow and directed her attention toward Chickie. "Lord Boughorpington, may I take it by your presence that you vouch for whatever plan the captain is about to suggest?"

Chickie gave Lady Mayor Somerset a tight smile. "I vouch for my dear friend, Captain Tereshchenko. I can't vouch for her plan, because I haven't the faintest idea how it's actually going to work. The whole thing seems dreadful to me."

"I suppose that will have to do. Let me hear your plan, Captain Tereshchenko."

Svetlana took a deep breath. "We'd like to drain the Somerset Cask into a new receptacle, outside of your uncle's basement. That way, we can bring the Cranglimmering back to you."

Lady Mayor Somerset frowned. "What will that do to the quality of the whiskey?"

"If we manage it correctly, very little," Annette replied. "I don't anticipate that any of the coopers in Merrowbarrow have a new barrel large enough to rehome the entirety of the Cranglimmering. But if we transfer it into smaller barrels, they'll be easier to store."

"So you drain the whiskey from the large cask into the smaller ones, and then what? Disassemble the whole thing to get the information you seek?"

"No, we've got a different idea for that as well," Svetlana said. "The pressure of the liquid inside the cask may be helping your uncle's former basement remain intact, and that might be contributing to holding Merrowbarrow up, at least in part. So we don't want to take it apart, nor keep it empty for too long. But we do need to see what's on the inside of the staves. So we think we can drill a hole in one end, big enough for our mechanic to crawl through. With some paper and some wax, he can take rubbings of the staves."

"And then refill it with rainwater afterwards," Lady Mayor Somerset said with a chuckle.

"Precisely."

The Lady Mayor nodded solemnly, her gaze fixed on the worn carpet beneath her feet. "This cannot wait until the landmass can be stabilized, can it?"

"It could," Svetlana admitted. "But if we wait, then we risk the possibility that others will realize that the Somerset Cask has been found. If we do this quietly, we may be able to keep it 'lost' for a little while longer."

"Regardless of your decision, I have already written a letter to send to the High Council to seek their assistance in stabilizing Merrowbarrow," Chickie said. "It awaits only your word, but they will certainly need to be involved."

Lady Mayor Somerset's frown grew deeper. "Perhaps it is simply time that we leave this place, and let it crumble into the ocean. It is already so near to collapse."

"The engineers may determine that to be the case, in the end," Annette said softly. "But it's worth seeing what can be salvaged."

That seemed to assuage Lady Mayor Somerset's concerns, and she nodded. "Then drain the cask and send your mechanic in, though I would not wish that task on anyone. I should like a copy of the rubbings your mechanic makes."

Svetlana tensed. They were hardly in a position to say no, but the thought of pieces of the Long-Cursed Map being out in the wind was a reason for concern, even if the ghost ship and the Republic had already sought the Somerset Cask and gone away empty handed. If the High Council sent engineers to stabilize Merrowbarrow, they'd be sure to come across the staves sooner rather than later. But a stray copy of the information could fall into anyone's hands. "May I ask what for?"

"I do not intend to share the information they contain. I simply wish to chronicle them amongst the holdings of my family. Call it a footnote in the family history that I have been composing for the past thirty-five years, trying to find answers to the strange insanity that overcame Uncle Edwyn. I assure you I will keep them secure. If that is amenable, then I grant my permission to enact this plan."

Svetlana nodded. She hoped she would not come to regret this decision. "Copy of the rubbings for your archives. Done."

# CHAPTER TEN

"This is basically the worst plan ever, Sveta," Athos grumbled, just loud enough for Svetlana to hear him.

"Taking it out of the rock would be worse," she snapped back. "Jo and I are going to keep the ship steady right beneath the cask while Indy and Deliah go in. If the rock collapses, or the bottom falls out of the cask, we'll catch them."

"And if that destabilizes a bigger chunk of the city, and we wind up with tons of rock on deck?"

"I'm open to alternative plans, Athos. This is the best we've got."

Indigo and Deliah stepped onto the bridge, both wearing hastily constructed headlamps on bands encircling their heads. Deliah clutched a bag filled to bursting with dark colored candles, while Indigo held a large roll of paper beneath his arm.

Svetlana smiled at the teenagers. "Ready?"

"Once there's no more whiskey, yes," Indigo said. "But it's going to smell bad."

"We think that the hole you use to get in there will help air it out. And the quicker you work, the sooner we can get you back on board."

Indigo nodded, while Deliah edged closer to him. The girl had been fairly quiet since coming onboard *The Silent Monsoon*, at least in the presence of the rest of the crew. She and Indigo chattered nearly nonstop when they were alone in the engine room, the musical sounds of their voices filtering up through the floorboards of the bridge at all hours. Svetlana wasn't entirely sure that either of the teenagers slept half a wink.

Annette poked her head through the bridge door. "That's the last of the Cranglimmering. The Lady Mayor's carpenter is carving the hole now."

Svetlana looked out at the ten small barrels of Cranglimmering arrayed across the deck. With the Bartram Cask rumored at a value of a million Quinpence, any one of those casks would fetch 100,000 Quinpence, assuming the contents could be verified. And a part of her still thought that might be the better deal, in the long run. She didn't want the Gem of the Seas. The rest of the Last Emperor's Hoard might be worth substantially more than even all of the remaining Cranglimmering in the world. The responsibility of being the one to find and hold the Gem of the Seas was daunting, but those who wanted the power that it afforded were the least likely to use it responsibly, she feared.

A clatter of a wooden disk on the deck of *The Silent Monsoon* broke her reverie. The carpenter that Lady Mayor Somerset had sent over to the ship descended his ladder soon after and nodded at the teenagers.

Annette took Indigo's paper and Deliah's bag, and Indigo began climbing the ladder. Deliah watched him go up, and then followed. Once both of them had vanished from Svetlana's line of sight, Annette climbed up a few rungs and handed up the paper and bag. Then she came back inside the bridge.

"And now, we wait," Annette said.

"I hate waiting," Svetlana grumbled.

A hail of small stones pelted the roof of the bridge, and Annette turned to Athos. "We might want to get those barrels under cover, just in case something big comes down."

"Would have been great to think about that before they started bouncing around inside the cask, don't you think?" Athos asked.

"Yes, but she's right," Svetlana said. "Jo, can you hold the position without me?"

Jo nodded. "We're more or less anchored here. A gale force wind might cause us some trouble, but it's been pretty still since we arrived at Merrowbarrow. Go ahead, Cap'n. Have fun dodging the rocks."

Svetlana, Annette, and Athos left the bridge, each scanning the jagged rock above them for impending collapse. Some of the stone still showed marks from the tools that had been used to carve away the mountain that had once surrounded it, but more looked as though pieces had been crumbling away for decades. The edges of the original Somerset Cask were visible just above, where a chunk of the brickwork had been cleared away, and a burst of giggles emanated from it.

"More work, less playing," Svetlana called up toward the cask.

"Yes, Captain," Indigo replied, his high-pitched voice eerie with the echoes of the cask around him.

"Alright," Svetlana said. "Annette, duck down into the hold, and Athos and I will bring the casks to you."

Athos opened his mouth as if to protest, but then nodded. "Good call. Keep the doc safe."

"Exactly," Svetlana said.

Annette grinned. "Much obliged." She went below as Athos and Svetlana began turning the barrels onto their sides and rolling them toward the stairs that led into the hold.

Above them, a gasp rang out from the cask. Svetlana couldn't tell for certain which of the teenagers it had been. "Indy, are you alright?"

"Heard some rumbles," Indigo said.

"Could it be your stomach?" Svetlana suggested.

"Maybe. Can we eat?"

"When you've got all of the staves copied." She paused at the foot of the ladder. "How many do you see with lines on them?"

"One, two, three—" Indigo's voice trailed off. "Six. And four with words."

"Words?" Svetlana asked. Her mind whirled. Lady de Whittvy hadn't mentioned words on any of the staves, just the map of the continents at they had been before the Boiling. Somehow, it seemed unlikely that any words found inside the cask would be unimportant. "Make rubbings of those as well, Indy. Anything that looks like map lines or words."

"One done," Deliah sang out.

"Nine more to go," Svetlana replied as she returned to rolling barrels across the deck.

As she and Athos handed the last barrel down to Annette, the entire deck pitched. Svetlana lost her footing and plummeted toward the stairs, but Athos grabbed her arm as she began to fall.

"Gotcha," he said with a smile.

"About time you saved me from something," Svetlana replied, sharing his grin. "Though I do wonder why we just pitched like that." She glanced down below. "Annette, you alright?"

"Just lost my balance a moment. All the barrels are safe too. You want me to bundle them all together, just in case?"

"Wouldn't be the worst plan in the world."

"I'll help her get them set," Athos said.

Svetlana nodded. "Stay below unless we call you up to the bridge, then. It'll be safer." She hurried back onto the bridge, dodging a stone about the size of her fist that pelted the deck beside her, cracking the plank it struck.

"Sorry about that wiggle, Cap'n," Jo said as soon as she saw Svetlana. "There's a chunk of rock over the stern that's looking mighty loose to me. I wanted to see how much play I could get in our position without disturbing the ladder."

Looking back out onto the deck, Svetlana frowned. "I'd feel a lot better about this situation if the ladder falling wasn't even an option. I'm gonna bring it down. If worse comes to worse, it's not so far of a jump down to the roof that it would hurt the kids."

"They're both made of rubber anyway, I think," Jo said.

Svetlana stepped back out onto the deck, again watching for falling rocks. The teenagers had gone silent in the cask above, though she heard the faint sound of rubbing. "Indy? I'm going to take down the ladder for right now. We'll put it back up when you're done, okay? We just don't want it to get knocked down."

"Okay," Deliah replied.

Svetlana hesitated. "Is Indy alright?"

"Both fine," Deliah said. "Just busy working."

"Alright, then. When you're all done, drop down some of those candle stubs, and we'll come back out to get you down."

"Aye, aye, Captain," Deliah said.

~

A knock on Svetlana's cabin door woke her the next morning, or at least what she thought of as morning. Her pocket watch said otherwise, giving a time of quarter past noon.

"What is it?" she called out as she sat up in bed and stretched.

"Message from Lar," Annette replied through the door. "Did I wake you?"

Svetlana yawned. "Yeah. Feel like we've been burning the candle at both ends lately."

"Apparently that's common to Rrusadon," Annette said. "You decent?"

Straightening her oversized shirt and pulling on a pair of loose trousers, Svetlana opened the door. "Am now. What's the hurry?"

Annette held out a small folded note. "Don't know yet, but the messenger insisted it was important that you get this right away."

Svetlana unfolded the note and read it aloud. "Come by Warehouse 17 when you're awake. We can talk dinner plans then."

"Dinner plans?"

With a shrug, Svetlana replied, "I guess he misses me."

"And do you miss him?" Annette asked with a chuckle.

"I'm trying to not get too attached. I told him as much, and he agreed to it. I think I'm better at it than he is, to my immense surprise."

Annette rolled her eyes. "Of course, Captain. Do you want me to wake anyone else?"

Svetlana looked at the note again. "Since we don't know what we're going to see, I don't see any reason to. At least not yet."

"Then I'll let you get dressed and—" Annette waved her hands in the direction of Svetlana's head. "—do something with your hair."

"Five minutes," Svetlana said.

~

Twenty minutes later, Svetlana and Annette stood inside of Warehouse 17, jaws slack. The wall in front of them had been covered with wooden slats, much like the ones in Lady de Whittvy's map room. Though Lady de Whittvy's slats had been etched by her probability machine, the ones here on Rrusadon had been painted with both the map of the world as it looked today in white, and narrow black lines that indicated the pieces of the map that Svetlana and her crew had located. And though the Kavisolis didn't have Lady de Whittvy's probability machine in the warehouse, they had something the scientist had not had—he data from five sets of staves.

Lar beamed at Svetlana and Annette. "We've been working on this since we got back from Bonebriar. The data from your friend

Lady de Whittvy's film was a good start. We were able to reproduce the staves from the Silver Cask precisely, and the rubbings you brought back from Merrowbarrow matched up well enough that I put a crew to work as soon as you returned."

"This is amazing, Lar," Svetlana said. "I only wish I knew whether the film included the Bartram Cask staves as well."

"Unlikely, according to my men," Lar said. "But we now know that not all of the casks had the same number of inscribed staves. The Silver Cask had seven, while the Somerset Cask had ten."

"And how many did Lady de Whittvy's data account for?" Annette asked.

"Fourteen."

Svetlana closed her eyes tightly and rubbed at her temples. She could almost picture the map room at Lady de Whittvy's house on Bonebriar, but her memories of that room were heavily colored by the things that had happened there and less of the décor, as important as it was. She could clearly recall Lady de Whittvy being dragged from the room by ghostly pirates, and her own panic in that moment, dealing with assailants she couldn't stop. Thinking of the room also brought back her final argument with Bobby—she still smarted from the realization that one of her oldest friends was not the man she thought he was—but the map itself was hazy.

"She may have had more," Svetlana finally said, opening her eyes again. "I can't say for certain." She approached the wall and examined a pair of staves on the right-hand side. Hints of a flowery script teased at words, but no definitive words were apparent yet. "Indy mentioned that there was writing on the inside of the Somerset Cask. Do you know if this is one of them?"

Lar moved beside Svetlana and wrapped one arm around her waist. With his other arm, he pointed at a small letter "B" at the top of the stave in question. "We've coded the two new ones—the Silver Cask is 'A', and the Somerset Cask is 'B'. We have no way of determining which staves came from the original three casks, unfortunately."

Svetlana shook her head, leaning into Lar's shoulder. "I don't know that it matters that much, because none of them seem to have any writing on them." She frowned. "But they should, wouldn't you think? Down here in the Southern Sea?"

"It's possible. Did Lady de Whittvy's map have writing on it that wasn't reproduced on the film?"

"No, it didn't. But I'm wondering if the original staves had little enough writing that it didn't register as such." She chuckled. "Hard to believe that a super genius would miss a detail like that, but if she wasn't entirely sure what she was looking at, I could see it seeming unimportant. No writing in the Silver Cask?"

Lar brushed aside Svetlana's hair to whisper into her ear. "I'm having my men double check. Promise you won't tell the Lord Mayor that we reopened his cask?"

"My lips are sealed," Svetlana replied with a smile. "For now, at least."

"What are you two going on about?" Annette asked.

Svetlana glanced over her shoulder, her good eye sparkling. "Dinner plans."

"Right," Annette said. "So shall I go fetch anyone else from the ship?"

"Not yet," Svetlana said. "This is all useful to have, but until we get more staves, it still doesn't tell us where the treasure is. It just tells us many places where the treasure isn't."

"Which is valuable," Lar said. "But not enough for you to go jetting off to look for it yet."

Svetlana arched her eyebrow at him, a smile still playing across her lips. "Are you holding back information to keep us here longer?"

"I would not dream of such a deception," he said, his eyes glittering as he shared her smile. "If I had, I wouldn't have shown you this map at all."

"Right, then," Annette said. "I'll leave you two to flirting, and I'll head back to the ship."

Svetlana disentangled herself from Lar and hurried over to Annette. "We need to find the Gyrfalcon Cask."

"Then I'll hit the books for a bit." Annette smiled. "Go have some fun while we've got the time."

~

The look on Annette's face when Svetlana stumbled into the mess the next morning told the captain everything she needed to know.

"Nothing?"

"Nothing. It's all 'the Gyrfalcons this' and 'the Gyrfalcons that,' but nothing useful about where they might have stashed a cask."

Svetlana shook her head as she helped herself to tea. By the time she had returned to the table, Athos had emerged from his room, making a beeline for the tea pan as well.

"So we've got no lead on the Gyrfalcon Cask, and unless Indy can get Drassilis functioning again, nothing on the Bartram Cask either."

"And we can't be certain that the automaton has anything on the Bartram Cask," Athos said. "You're assuming that Lady de Whittvy bothered to share any secrets she might have learned before her untimely demise with her 'son.'"

"So a sandbar and a coral reef, huh?" Svetlana said. "If we had somewhere to fly, we could work on Drassilis while we look for the Gyrfalcon Cask. But with no leads, we've got no reason to leave. And that means we have no idea if the Air Fleet or the ghosts are getting closer to the Gyrfalcon Cask."

Jo's loud yawn announced her entrance into the room. "What do the ghosts want, anyway?"

"To find the casks?" Svetlana asked with a shrug.

"Sure, but why?" Jo replied.

Svetlana frowned. "I don't ... I'm not sure. I think Mirage was the first one who mentioned the ghost ship to me, and he told me to beware it, like there was just one ghost ship. But that was when he was strung out on ether."

"Okay, but that's a place to start," Annette said, flipping open her journal to a blank page. She wrote "ghost ship" in her tidy script at the top of the sheet, and beneath that, "Mirage, on ether."

"Then the ghosts abducted Lady de Whittvy from the map room." Svetlana chewed at her lip while she breathed the warm and slightly bitter smell from her mug of tea. "I don't think they were there long enough to get any information from the map, but they might have gotten some from her."

"And you said that Lady Mayor Somerset spoke with the ghosts?" Annette asked, frowning. "That is not a sentence I ever anticipated saying."

Athos shook his head. "Didn't speak with them, exactly. She said that the ghosts spoke to her long-dead uncle, not her. Which is also a strange sentence to say aloud."

"Okay, but we're skipping a step or three," Jo said. "We know that ghost ships paid visits to the locations of some, if not all, of the casks prior to or after taking Lady de Whittvy. So ghost ships made a tour of potential cask locations. Took Lady de Whittvy. Maybe visited some more locations. Kidnapped Lord Mayor Silver. Right?"

"Right," Svetlana said. "But Lord Mayor Silver wouldn't give up the location of his cask, which means, as best as I can tell, we're the only ones with that information. The ghosts couldn't find it, and there's also no reason to suspect the Air Fleet has managed to find it either. Especially since we know exactly where that one is."

"That one and the Somerset Cask," Athos reminded her. "So we've found two casks they haven't."

"That we have," Annette said. "At least until we consider the writing that dear old Lady de Whittvy didn't catch. We have to assume that since the High Council has the actual physical staves for three casks, while we've only had access to the physical staves of two casks, they've logically got more of the writing than we do. So they're up three to two on that count."

"If the writing even matters," Svetlana reminded her. "So far, we can't say that it does or doesn't."

"And yet we still haven't gotten to the point," Jo said through clenched teeth. Athos hurriedly set her tea mug in front of her, the tea within the customary creamy brown that was the way she liked it. "What. Does. The. Ghost. Ship. Want?"

Svetlana leaned back in her chair and considered. "They want the map, most likely, just like the High Council and us. I think the question we should be asking is why."

"Yes, that too," Jo said. She blew across the top of her mug and gulped down a small sip. "Who are the ghosts working for?"

"Not us," Athos said. "And odds are, not the Air Fleet either. So they're a third party. Neutral party. Only, probably not actually neutral."

Looking up from her journal page, now covered with assorted notes, Annette whispered, "The only person we know who might be able to answer that question is in our engine room right now."

"Deliah," Svetlana breathed, her eye widening. "She's been on a ghost ship or two."

"But if we all go marching down there and demanding answers, she's likely to clam up," Annette said.

Jo nodded. "She trusts you best, Cap'n. May as well use that to your advantage."

Svetlana nodded. "Though we've been down this road before. She said the ghosts are just looking for the casks like we are, and that they told her they had already found them all, but we know that to be a lie, seeing as they didn't know where to find the Silver Cask or the Somerset Cask."

"Then I suppose the question might be what else they told her that was lies," Athos suggested.

# CHAPTER ELEVEN

The engine room was just as humid as Rrusadon, though it smelled more of oil and burnt coal than plant life. Svetlana lingered in the doorway, not wanting to commit to stepping into the sauna-like space if she could avoid it. "Indy? Deliah? You in there?"

"Yes, Captain," Deliah sang out.

"Why's it so humid in here?"

"Had to vent a boiler," Indigo replied. "For Drassilis."

Svetlana took a step inside. "Are you making progress?"

"Some," Indigo said, an apparition coming from the cloud within the engine room, directly in front of Svetlana. He cocked his head to the side, his blue hair nearly as curly as Athos's hair in the humidity. "I think you're melting."

"That's because the air here is more steam than air. Can you and Deliah come on deck? I wanted to ask her more questions about the ghost ship."

Deliah made a disgusted noise from somewhere within the engine room. "They don't have the right ghosts."

Svetlana peered into the steam. Deliah had said the same thing when they found her at Heatbourne. "Right, the nice ghosts. Have the nice ghosts ever been on a ghost ship?"

"Sometimes," Deliah said, peering at her boots and avoiding Svetlana's gaze. "The mean ghosts are scary, so the ghost ships take them first."

"So wait, the ghost ships, or the crews of the ghost ships, pick and choose what ghosts they take? How does that work?"

Deliah shrugged.

"Not all the ghosts have a home," Indigo said, cocking his head to the side.

It wasn't a question, but Deliah nodded all the same.

"So you've been to the … what is it, the ghost world?" Svetlana asked. "Or is that just the Aether? Is that where the ghosts live, in the Aether?"

"I think so," Deliah said. "Ghost live in the Aether. I've been in the Aether. Both."

Svetlana pulled her monocular from her eye and rubbed at the bridge of her nose. She wasn't getting anywhere with this line of questioning. "Who decides which ghosts are nice and mean?"

"Me, I guess." Deliah shrugged and stared at her boots again. "And the ghost ships have mostly mean ghosts."

"Okay. So nice ghosts aren't on the ghost ships, and mean ghosts are. Got it." Svetlana rolled her shoulders backward, trying to release some of the tension this conversation was causing. "I just need to know if there's anything else you heard while you were onboard the ghost ship that might have to do with the casks. We know that the ghosts haven't found them all yet, regardless of what they may have pretended. Do you know who they might be working for, or why they want to find the casks?"

Deliah shook her head, her bright orangish-yellow braids bobbing on either side of her head. "I'm sorry, Captain. Mean ghosts aren't helpful." She frowned suddenly.

"What is it?" Indigo asked, taking Deliah's slender hand in his.

"One ghost said something about Heliopolis and the Aetherwhere Division."

Svetlana frowned. She'd never heard of an Aetherwhere Division, but she wondered what the Air Fleet might name a division where people who had encountered ghosts and ghost ships collected information. People like her ex-girlfriend, Captain Narcissa Marsh, who had spent years in just such a place. She gasped. "The what? The Aetherwhere Division?"

Deliah nodded. "At the Air Fleet Headquarters."

"Did they say anything more about it?" Svetlana asked, her mind already awhirl.

"The next best source." Deliah frowned. "Didn't say what the best source was. I'm sorry, Captain."

Svetlana shook her head. "No, this is good! Thank you, Deliah! I think you may have just solved one of our problems." She peered past the teenagers. With the door to the engine room open, much of the collected steam had dissipated, and she could see the heap of parts that was Drassilis. "Keep working on the automaton, alright?"

"Can I bring him back up to the mess?" Indigo asked.

"If that's where you think you need to work on him, Indy. But no more trying to power him from the cook stove, okay?"

Indigo shrugged. "Alright. His batteries should all be recharged by now, I guess."

"Great," Svetlana said. "Keep up the good work." Turning from the engine room, she ran back toward the crew quarters and the mess.

Athos called out from the mess. "What's the rush, Sveta?"

"We need to get an airwave to Narci," Svetlana said, ducking through the doorway.

Athos scrunched his eyes shut and turned his head to one side. "Have you gone mad?" he asked through clenched teeth.

"Probably. But Deliah said that the ghost ship was interested in what was happening at the Aetherwhere Division at Headquarters."

Athos opened his eyes and turned back to Svetlana. "Wait, Aetherwhere Division? Is that the secret program in the basement of the Academy?"

"I think it might be."

"And you want to talk to Narci about that?"

"No. About the Gyrfalcons. The Aetherwhere Division just reminded me that her roommate, when we were cadets, was part of that program too—they always joked about going to the dungeon—but her roommate was also a Gyrfalcon."

"How in the abyss do you plan on contacting Narci and not having her go straight to Bobby? Or someone else at the Fleet?"

Svetlana grinned. "That's the part I need your help with. We need to concoct a message that will tell Narci how much I need to see her, and on somewhere other than Heliopolis, and we need to make the message so obscure that only she'll know that I'm the one sending it."

Athos threw his hands up. "Sure, nothing complicated. Just an airwave message filled with nuance and symbolism. That'll be like a stroll after Lift."

"If anyone can do it—" Svetlana said, trailing off into a broad grin.

Athos stroked his goatee, not looking at Svetlana as he did. Finally, he shook his head. "Alright. But you're going to have to give me a lot of details. Where's the first place you kissed her?"

"On the lips?" Svetlana asked.

Athos crossed his arms over his chest and arched an eyebrow. "Where at the Academy?"

"Oh. Right. Under the clock tower archway."

"Good. Okay. I can work with this. 'Recall our day beneath the clock. I urgently wish to rekindle our spark. Tell me when and where.'"

Svetlana arched an eyebrow. "Can you concoct something that doesn't sound like I'm trying to get her in bed?"

"Coded messages between lovers are a time-honored tradition," Athos said. "Chickie would be with me on this. You send a message like that, and she'll answer. Actually, we'll want Chickie to send the message. If it comes from Rrusadon direct to Narci, this place will be crawling with Air Fleet in hours."

"You don't think it'll be suspicious arriving from Chickie to Narci?"

Athos shrugged. "Who are we to judge what the nobility does in their extensive free time? Anyway, I'm sure Chickie and Narci have loads in common. Like ... well ... looking good in green?"

Svetlana just shook her head. "Whatever you say, Athos. Just make the meeting happen, one way or another?"

"Oh, I will. That's what I do. I bring people together." He looked at her. "If you want to change my message, I'm open to suggestions."

"I don't want to give her the wrong idea. Can we make it a sound a little less flirtatious?"

"Alright," Athos said. "If we're pretending it's from Chickie to Narci, how about, 'There is a timely matter about which I must consult you.' We'll send a separate message to Chickie to let him know what we're doing. Then they can make the arrangements together, and Chickie will tell us when and where. Better?"

"Much," Svetlana agreed.

~

Toffinghollow was on a broad open plain near Bluesummer. The thought of being so close to a city like Bluesummer mad

Svetlana feel like someone was bound to be watching her, but it was the place Narcissa had suggested for their rendezvous. And it did have the advantage of being far enough from Heliopolis that so long as Narci wasn't planning to sell them out, they'd be far away from the prying eyes of the Air Fleet.

Still, Svetlana had told Jo to fly *The Silent Monsoon* in a path around the edges of the island that housed Bluesummer and Toffinghollow. She wanted her distinctive balloons far out of sight of any ships that Narci might have brought with her. So she sat in an arguably reputable tavern in Toffinghollow, waiting.

She wasn't alone, of course. Athos lurked in another part of the tavern, a broad, floppy hat brim masking most of his face. So long as he stuck to the shadows and didn't speak, Narci might never realize he was there.

A slight young girl with tawny skin and golden-brown hair, dressed in something that looked more like a fancy dressing gown than the sort of clothing that one wore outdoors, slipped through the doorway and made a beeline for Svetlana. Svetlana tensed. She hadn't bothered with any disguise, because Toffinghollow was far enough outside of their typical routes that no one here should know of her.

"I have a message for you," the girl said, her words sliding in a child's lisp.

Svetlana leaned close to the girl, smiling as she did. "Is it a good message or a bad message?"

The girl cocked her head to the side, considering. "Good, I think. There's someone who wants to talk to you outside."

Svetlana glanced at Athos, who had tilted his hat enough to one side that she could catch his gaze. She arched an eyebrow, and then looked toward the doorway.

He nodded in response, but stayed in his seat.

"Did the person give you a name?"

The girl shook her head, straight hair shifting like a curtain around her round face. "She gave me this, though," she said, holding up a copper coin stamped with the crest of the city of Heliopolis.

Svetlana frowned. Though the coin had likely come from Narci, it still gave her pause. A clearer sign from Narci might have been a piece of Air Fleet ephemera, but the errand girl would not have accepted such as payment. The coin bearing the Heliopolis crest almost felt like Narcissa was taunting Svetlana. She'd just have to grit her teeth and take it, she decided, rising from the table and ruffling the little girl's hair. "Thank you, that's as good as a name." *I hope.*

Across the street from the tavern, a slender woman lounged on the porch of a ramshackle building. She, too, wore an enormous hat that concealed most of her face, but Svetlana recognized her build in an instant and made her way across the street to talk to Narci.

As Svetlana approached, Narcissa looked up from beneath her hat. Worry lines creased Svetlana's former lover's dark skin, but Narcissa forced a smile. "It's good to see you again."

"Likewise," Svetlana said, her gaze darting around at the few passersby on the narrow street through the town. "You feel up for a walk?"

Narci rose and looked toward the tavern. "I'd rather walk than go inside, that's for certain. But who are we leaving behind inside?"

"Athos," Svetlana said, not bothering to conceal the fact from Narcissa. The two women knew each other too well. "And who'd you bring?"

"Just a pilot—no one who would know you. He's not even Fleet. He's at the tea house on the next block over until I retrieve him."

Svetlana nodded tersely and gestured toward the outskirts of Toffinghollow. "Let's walk, then."

Narcissa fell into step beside Svetlana, and the two of them walked in silence. With no conscious effort, they matched their strides, Narci taking smaller steps to allow for Svetlana's shorter legs. It felt like old times, despite the years and events that had passed.

Svetlana breathed in the fresh air, laden with the scents of mown hay and livestock. Being on the islands always meant smells that overpowered the sulfurous ocean, for good or ill. She'd accept the smell of cow dung for a breath or two of air that didn't smell like a rotten egg.

"So. How did it go with your court martial?" Svetlana finally asked.

"Temporarily relieved of command. All indications so far tell me that temporary in this case means 'until she gives up and quits,' but they've got me doing busy work at Headquarters, and they're talking about having me work with some of the cadets." Narci shook her head, a faint laugh escaping her throat as she continued. "Me, teaching. Can you believe it?"

Svetlana chuckled. "Never saw that coming." She paused and took a breath, recomposing her expression. "I am sorry it came to that."

Narci shook her head, her stubby brown and silver dreadlocks bumping against her cheeks. "My troops shouldn't have fired on a civilian, and they knew better. The only reason I got court martialed for it was that your friend was apparently an enemy of the Republic."

Svetlana heard the tension in Narcissa's voice when she said "friend," but she didn't want to dwell on that. "So I take it I haven't hit that status yet?"

Narcissa didn't respond at first, but then said, "I don't know," in a quieter than normal voice.

Svetlana stopped and touched Narci's shoulder.

Narci turned, tears hovering in the corners of her eyes. "I haven't looked to find out," Narci said. "I don't want to know." She took a deep breath. "But that isn't why you sent me your message, is it? You need me for something else."

Svetlana shook her head. "Back when we were cadets, your roommate was Corinne Gyrfalcon."

Narci nodded, wiping her eyes and frowning. "Yes, what about her?"

"You stayed in touch, didn't you?"

"Yeah, we were both on the *Zweiflaggen* after graduation." Narci shrugged. "We went to Orwall for holiday skiing trips a couple of times. Why?"

Svetlana chewed at the inside of her lip. Now that she was at the point of the conversation where she could ask Narcissa about the Gyrfalcon Cask, she was hesitant. Narci had been forthcoming with information thus far, and she wasn't reacting like Svetlana was asking her questions that she didn't want to answer, ut now, turning the conversation to the casks, Svetlana didn't expect that the answers would come as easily. She suspected Narci would have to maintain Fleet secrets. If Narci did have the information Svetlana wanted, though, they'd have to part ways after Svetlana had that information as well, and she wasn't sure she was ready to say goodbye again.

Narcissa broke the silence first, her voice soft. "Oh, Sveta. Don't treat me like I haven't a clue what you're interested in. You want to know about the cask, I take it? The Gyrfalcon Cask?"

"How'd you—"

"That's all anyone wants to know about," Narcissa said, her voice hardening. "And I have no issue telling you exactly what I told every officer of the Fleet who's asked me. I don't know where it is. I never saw it. Corinne never told me where it was." Looking down, she clenched her hands into fists in front of her, and continued in a whisper. "But I will tell you the one piece I didn't give them." She met Svetlana's gaze, her own gaze steady. "Corinne told me about an aunt or some such of hers, who she called the keeper of the cask. Her name was Elwisia Gyrfalcon."

Svetlana watched Narcissa closely. Narci seemed genuine in her insistence on looking Svetlana in the eyes, not wavering in the slightest. She was telling the truth, even if Svetlana couldn't figure out why her former lover would be willing to share information with her that she hadn't shared with the Air Fleet. As Svetlana considered what Narci had said, she stumbled over one word. She cleared her throat, and asked, "Was?"

"Maybe still is. I'm not sure." Narci let out a long breath and relaxed her shoulders, clearly calmer now that she had given Svetlana this information. "I never met anyone named Elwisia, and the way the family talked about her ... I get the impression she was unpopular among the greater portion of the family. They spoke of her only in the harshest tones, and never for long. Corinne, I think she had been told that Elwisia was mad, and that the family just didn't acknowledge her anymore because of that." Narci shrugged. "There was a lot about the Gyrfalcons that I never understood, but Corinne and I stayed friends despite the odds."

"Why haven't you told the Air Fleet about Elwisia?" Svetlana watched Narci's dark brown eyes as she asked the question, ready to catch even the slightest twitch.

"Because all I had was the little bit of information Corinne had given me. It was nothing I could prove. And until the whole nonsense with Bonebriar? No one had ever asked me about my ties to the Gyrfalcons. I don't know what the Air Fleet wants with the Gyrfalcon Cask, and, really, I don't know what you want with it either. But at this point, I'd rather help you than them." Narci held Svetlana's gaze the entire time she spoke, without even a quiver.

She wasn't as stiff as she had been, but she clipped her words, like she was reporting to a superior officer.

Underlying that, Svetlana could detect anger, seething just beneath Narci's words. It wasn't directed at Svetlana. It was directed toward the Fleet and the way they'd only asked Narci questions about her past when it suited their purposes. Svetlana felt a twinge of guilt that she was doing the exact same thing to Narci that the Air Fleet had done. Before she could stop herself, she reached out her hand. "You don't have to go back. You can come with us."

Narci choked back a sob. "It's not always that easy, Sveta. What I want and what I have to do are two different things. And as appealing as running away is, that's not who I am." She squared her shoulders. "Anyway, if I go back to Headquarters, I may be able to get you more information. I take it that Lord Boughorppington can be trusted with messages for you?"

Svetlana nodded, tucking her hands behind her back so that she didn't continue reaching for Narci. "He'll insist you call him Chickie. But yes, he can be trusted."

Narci nodded. "I should go. My pilot will wonder why I've been gone so long." She paused and looked at Svetlana for a long moment. "Be careful, Sveta. I don't know what you're mixed up in—just be careful."

Svetlana didn't watch her go, as her good eye clouded over as badly as her blind eye and tears began to flow.

~

Svetlana managed to compose herself before retrieving Athos and heading back to the ship. They were silent as they walked. Athos didn't need to ask to know that Svetlana was troubled, and she appreciated not having to explain anything to him.

When they arrived on the bridge, Jo took one look at her and shook her head. "So nothing?"

"Not much," Svetlana replied. "Unless you know where to find someone called Elwisia Gyrfalcon. She's apparently the only one who knows where the family keeps their cask, and she's not too popular among the rest of the family."

"How's Narcissa?" Annette asked softly, placing her hand on Svetlana's shoulder as she spoke.

Svetlana shrugged and swallowed hard. "Surviving. Just like the rest of us."

After a moment, Athos said, "So I've got a crazy idea. We're not that far from Bluesummer. Why don't we do a fly-by? We could get lucky again."

Jo laughed. "Yeah, maybe they've worked their cask in to the design of their house somehow, and it'll be hidden in plain sight, just like the Somerset Cask."

That managed to elicit a chuckle from Svetlana, despite her melancholy after talking to her ex-lover. "Why not?" she said with a shrug. "Not sure we've got any better ideas at this point."

*The Silent Monsoon* took off, flying along the coast of the island that housed both Toffinghollow and Bluesummer. The inland areas were green, rolling hills, interspersed with broad plains like the one near Toffinghollow, while the coastline was jagged and brown. Far beneath the ship, the ocean roiled. Svetlana stared out at the water, imagining that it seemed even more tempestuous than normal. She wondered if it was just a reflection of her own mood.

The journey to the Gyrfalcon estate was brief, and Jo angled the ship toward the large house, arcing wide around the edges of the property. A flash of bright color caught Svetlana's eye, and she stared hard at the ground for another glimpse. A figure, dressed all in dark colors, but with a shock of wild ginger hair, stood below. Though she couldn't make out the person's face, Svetlana would have sworn that the person was looking straight at *The Silent Monsoon*.

"There's someone down there," Svetlana called out. "A ginger."

Annette and Athos joined Svetlana at the window.

"Sure looks like it," Athos said. "I think it's a woman, but the clothes are a bit too bulky to say for certain."

Drawing back from the window, Annette rubbed at her chin. "I just had an alarming thought. Are you certain Lady de Whittvy died?" Annette asked.

Svetlana gaped at Annette. "I didn't take her pulse, if that's what you're asking. I was a bit distraught at the time. But stranger things have happened. If it is her, and she's here, it must be for the Gyrfalcon Cask."

"So, are we landing to see if your dead scientist slash thief is still alive?" Jo asked.

Svetlana looked at Athos and Annette, both of whom nodded. "Yes, let's land out on the plain and see if we can find her before she runs off."

# CHAPTER TWELVE

"This place looks like no one has lived here in years," Athos said, frowning at the overgrown but browning lawn outside of the Gyrfalcon estate at Bluesummer. Multi-colored leaves had fallen from the few spindly trees, but the winds had pushed them up against the fencing in huge drifts. The house itself was sturdy stone, broader than it was tall, giving the impression of a fat snake stretched out to warm itself in the sun.

"Shuttered windows and capped chimneys," Annette said, pointing out those features. "It looks like they might just use it seasonally. Summer, I'd guess, if the name is to be believed."

Svetlana shivered in the cool air, made doubly brisk by standing in the shadow of the extensive Gyrfalcon manor house. "I'd hope it's a bit warmer here in summer. Their autumn is downright frigid."

"Let's just hope your mystery ginger hasn't decided to run off somewhere," Jo said, scanning the horizon with Indigo's goggles. "There are people working down in the vineyards to the south, and a few in some of the other fields here and there. Can't quite see all the way into the house with these, though." She tugged the goggles down, leaving them around her neck.

"Well, then I suppose we should knock on the front door," Svetlana said, striding in that direction and giving the door a solid rap. After waiting a minute, she tried the doorknob. "Locked."

Athos looked over the front of the house, then shrugged. "We could try for a different entrance. Maybe check the outbuildings first?"

Svetlana nodded. "You and Jo, me and Annette. Holler if you see anything." They made their way toward the back of the building, where half a dozen outbuildings sat, most squat cottages, along with a large barn. She paused. "Try not to get too distracted?"

Jo smirked. "Aye, Cap'n. I don't want to spend too much time here. Skyfather knows what the kids will be getting up to on the ship while we're gone."

"Fixing Drassilis, if we're lucky," Svetlana said. "You take the left, we'll take the right."

Svetlana and Annette moved toward the first cottage on their side of the outbuildings. The building was small enough that it had only window and door openings, not actual glass windows or even a door. The space inside was tidy, but had obviously suffered from exposure to the elements, the simple wooden furniture inside sun-bleached and worn to a soft finish by wind and rain. A spinning wheel leaned against what might have once been a rough bedframe, though the mattress and bedding were long gone.

"Servant quarters, you think?" Annette asked.

"Probably." Svetlana glanced back at the main house. "Though I suspect this spot would be much cooler in the evening, during the summer. They might have used the outbuildings for sleeping when the heat got too bad." She smiled. "My grandad liked to sleep on the porch when the house got too warm. Granmum liked it just fine, because then he wasn't snoring and keeping her up in the heat."

Annette looked around, tilting her head to the side to listen. Then she shook her head. "If there was anyone else here, I think we'd hear them."

"Don't forget Lady de Whittvy was a scientist and a thief. If it's her, she's probably going to be far quieter than we are."

"You said she got shot right in the chest though, didn't you?"

Svetlana nodded. "But she was wearing a corset. I've heard stories about women in corsets being shot, but the stays prevent the bullet from killing them."

Annette nodded. "Yes, I've even examined some women who were that lucky. But the majority aren't."

"I wish we'd been able to go back to get her body and give her a proper burial," Svetlana said. "Or find out that she wasn't actually dead."

Moving on to the next outbuilding, they found it to be almost identical to the first, only lacking a spinning wheel. The rough bedframe here retained more of its slats, almost making it look like it would be a reasonable, if a bit uncomfortable, place to take a nap.

Svetlana lingered in the door of this cottage, sniffing the air. "Do you smell smoke here?"

She moved out of the way to allow Annette access to the cottage. "A little, maybe." The doctor turned around and scanned the horizon, then pointed to a plume of white in the distance. "Might be smelling that, though."

Svetlana nodded, but glanced back at the small hearth in the cottage. "I just want to check." She stepped inside of the cottage and approached the hearth, placing her palm above the ashes below. Though no smoke rose from them, they radiated more warmth than an unused fireplace might. "Annette," she said, rising and turning back to the entrance.

Before she could say more, she noticed the woman crouched in the corner, dressed in a thick black hooded cloak that looked excessive for the cool autumn weather. Though most of the woman's face was covered, enough was visible that Svetlana was certain it wasn't Lady de Whittvy. "Who are you?"

"I could ask the same of you," the woman said, rising from her crouch. Her words were clipped, but her voice bore the unmistakable accent of someone who had been educated at the finest schools the Republic had to offer. "You're trespassing."

Svetlana arched an eyebrow. "And you're not?"

"That is correct." The woman tossed back the hood of her cloak, revealing cascading ginger curls framing a freckled face.

"Then you must be a Gyrfalcon," Svetlana said. She gave a curt bow. "Captain Svetlana Tereshchenko and Doctor Annette Campbell of *The Silent Monsoon*. We're looking for Elwisia Gyrfalcon."

"Whatever for?" the woman scoffed.

"She has answers that we're looking for."

"Such as?"

Svetlana considered the woman in front of her. The hooded cloak concealed both her figure and any possible weapons. Thus far, the woman had not behaved in a particularly threatening manner, but Svetlana was still wary. "I'd like to know who's asking, first. I gave you my name. It's only fair that you give me yours."

"I'm a Gyrfalcon. That should be good enough for a trespasser."

With a nod, Svetlana said, "As I said, we're looking for Elwisia Gyrfalcon, as we're told that she's the keeper of the Gyrfalcon Cask."

The woman laughed, though no mirth touched her eyes. "That old thing, eh? Does that explain why I've seen five airships in the past month that seemed to be taking the scenic route across my family's lands?"

"I wouldn't doubt it," Svetlana replied. "Seems that Cranglimmering has become a hot commodity lately."

The woman frowned, glancing away from Svetlana, then shook her head. "I'm afraid I can't help you, there."

Svetlana watched the woman closely. "It seems like you know something about your family's Cranglimmering, then?"

"I might, but I still don't know why you want to find it. You don't seem to know the history of it, if you're asking after it here."

"There's history, then? Would you be willing to share it?"

"What are you offering?" the woman said, crossing her arms over her chest.

Svetlana shrugged. "We've got fresh food on our ship. If you're not used to seeing many airships, that makes me think you're living on dried goods."

Her shoulders slumping, the woman said, "Well, you're not wrong about that. Bring me your offering, and we'll see what it's worth."

~

The inside of the barn, where the red-haired woman had led the crew members from *The Silent Monsoon*, was nothing like the outside suggested. No animals resided inside, the floors had been swept clean of any hay or other debris, and furniture roughly divided the large space into a sitting area and a dining area, with a curtained area in the hayloft that appeared to be a bedroom.

The woman dug through the crate that Svetlana had brought back from the ship. It hadn't been much, but judging by the expression on the woman's face, it was more fresh food than she had seen in a long time. On opening one tin of tea, she breathed deep of its scent, ran her fingers across the dried leaves, and gave the crew a smile, the first true one they'd seen from her.

122

While the woman continued to examine the other items in the crate, Annette leaned down to whisper into Svetlana's ear. "Have you had a look at this table?"

"I didn't know we were furniture shopping," Svetlana said, raising her left eyebrow.

She followed Annette to the table in question. It was a long, wide plank table, the sort that large families might eat around. Svetlana hadn't taken much note of it when they first entered the barn, but now that she was standing beside it, she realized that the planks all bowed inward, as though the table itself was a piece of a sizeable whiskey cask.

Athos stood off to one side, scribbling in a small pocket notebook. He caught Svetlana's good eye and smiled, and she moved to join him.

"Doc's got amazing eyes, don't you think?" he murmured.

Svetlana stifled a laugh as she peeked at what he was drawing. It wasn't a portrait of the doctor, as someone overhearing his comment might suspect, but rather a sketch of a carved and blackened portion of the wood at one end of the table. "That she does, Athos. Some of the best."

When Svetlana looked back toward the young woman, she was staring in the captain's direction. "I see you've noticed my table."

Svetlana nodded. "It's a rather unique piece, I daresay."

"I'm afraid you won't find much else like it around here. Or anywhere, really."

"It says a bit about the Gyrfalcons, to have such a thing on display," Annette said. She had positioned herself on Svetlana's left, just a bit ahead of her, and shot the captain a quick look to verify that they were thinking along similar lines.

"You'd hardly believe how we came by it, if I told you," the woman replied.

"Would you, then?" Svetlana asked, leaning against the edge of the table. "If I recall our bargain correctly, the offer was food for a tale."

The young woman stared hard at Svetlana. "You hardly strike me as antique collectors."

"Not antiques," Svetlana replied. "We're just folks of rarified tastes."

"Well, I most certainly cannot help you there. But I will tell you the story of this table. Sit." She approached the table, pulled out the chair nearest the marking that Athos had been sketching, draping her arms across it to block it from view.

The young woman chewed at her lip as the crew took seats around the table, not making eye contact with any of them. Finally she turned to look at Svetlana. "Five years ago, my cousins and I were bored. Our parents had brought out the cask for its yearly inspection and sampling—something they had done since it came into their possession. But afterward, they went off to catch up with one another—our family is somewhat far flung these days, and left the teenagers with nothing to do." She smiled. "Did you see the long slope outside the front of the house?"

"The one that goes down to the vineyards?" Jo asked.

"That one, yes. We tried to pump some water down it in order to make a mudslide, but there wasn't nearly enough to go very far. One of my cousins dared me to pull the plug from the cask, which was aimed down the hill." Her eyes sparkled. "We had a magnificent mudslide. But we also drained the cask entirely, and crashed through the fence and into the vineyard. That land, those crops, didn't belong to our family, and their owners were livid."

Annette chuckled softly, though it was a sad sound. "So the whiskey is gone. All of it. It's a pity whiskey isn't known to improve soil yields, or the crops that grow there."

Svetlana nodded. Though she didn't have much of a taste for the Cranglimmering herself, the thought of a million Quinpence turned into a mudslide pained her deeply.

"Indeed." The young woman shrugged. "At the time, we had no idea of its value. It was just, in our view, a stupid reason to have to come to Bluesummer every year, when we would rather be vacationing with our friends."

"Spoiled children do make the worst decisions," Athos said. "Trust me on that."

"Indeed, and we were spoiled more than most."

"So what happened after that?" Annette asked.

"Our family paid restitution to the vineyard owner," the young woman said, her expression growing dark, "and since my cousins all blamed me, as I had been the one who actually pulled the plug, the family told me I was to remain here and maintain the estate."

"Then you are Elwisia Gyrfalcon?" Svetlana asked. "Keeper of your family's cask, in a manner of speaking?"

The young woman nodded. "You've found me out. The title is to remind me of my lapse in judgement."

"What became of the cask itself? The staves?"

Elwisia tapped her fingers on the wood. "We reused some of them here. Some in the vineyard fence. We sold the rest, as lumber of that size and durability was at a premium at the time."

"Sold." Athos shook his head. "Long gone."

"Yes, but one of my tasks was to make an accounting of where all of the pieces went," Elwisia replied. "The ledgers are in the manor house. I can show you the few staves we have here, and then we can look at the ledgers."

"Have you any guess as to how many are here and how many were sold?" Svetlana asked.

Elwisia shook her head. "Thirty or forty, I think. I'm afraid I haven't looked at the ledgers for some time. And I did not make an accounting of any designs on the wood," she said, looking toward Athos. "I thought them to be the work of wood weevils or something of the sort. They are apparently of interest to you?"

Svetlana nodded. "They are. Knowing where the rest of your staves have wound up will help our little art project."

"What are they?" Elwisia asked, staring hard at Svetlana again.

Svetlana studied Elwisia. With every new person she told about the Long-Cursed Map, the odds of word spreading widely increased, but there was still more information to be gleaned from the staves of the Gyrfalcon Cask, and refusing to share information with Elwisia now might cause her to withhold information from them as well. "A map of the world before the Boiling. Some people believe the map to be cursed."

Elwisia tilted her head to the side, her eyes glittering in the lamplight within the barn. "I will give you the information that you want, but I require something else in return."

"More food?" Jo asked.

Svetlana held out a hand to silence Jo. While she similarly hoped that the request would not be to dip further into their dwindling fresh provisions, she wanted to hear Elwisia's request before dismissing it out of hand. "What would you require?"

"Books," Elwisia said. "I've read everything here a dozen times, and my family will not indulge me further. Give me the ones you've already read. The more adventure and excitement, the better!"

~

Back on *The Silent Monsoon*, with Elwisia's list and sketches of the small markings they had seen on two of the staves in hand, Svetlana felt good about their exchange. Annette had brought Elwisia a box of books, and Elwisia had given Annette a few books that were new to the doctor. In addition to that amicable arrangement, they'd made significant progress toward finding the remaining staves of the Gyrfalcon Cask. Though they would still not have any of the data from the Bartram Cask unless Drassilis had that information stored somewhere in his memory banks, having six out of seven casks worth of information would likely be sufficient to determine what they needed to do next.

"We're going to need a plan before we go running down all these staves willy-nilly," Jo said. "Or we need to go back to Rrusadon to see if your boyfriend can give us some coal."

"Isn't there any to be had here?" Annette asked.

"Plenty to be had," Jo replied. "It's the buying it that's a bit tight at the moment."

Since they'd started on this quest to track down the casks, Svetlana hadn't bothered with finding other work for the crew, and they'd incurred many expenses, draining their coffers. "Athos, you want to go see if we can get any cargo here? Something on the way to Langdale, Thorpes, or Crullfeld. Or Rrusadon if it comes to it."

Athos nodded and ducked out of the mess. In the corner, Indigo and Deliah poked at Drassilis's still dismantled body, chattering softly to one another as they worked.

Svetlana unrolled a map on the table, then went into the kitchen to pull down a few tins of spices and tea to use as place markers. "Alright, we've got staves in Langdale, Thorpes, Crullfeld, and Heliopolis at known locations. We've also got some that were used to build a ship for Dargon's Deliveries—"

"So you're looking at something like *The Sky Angels* or *Scarlet Seashell*," Jo said. "Maybe Dargon commissioned one or two more around then, but I know he's lost a couple of ships in the past couple of years too." She frowned. "So the staves could have wound up anywhere, if they were on one of the lost ships."

"You know this Dargon?" Annette asked.

"A little," Jo said, smiling slyly. "I worked for him a couple of times on below the boards jobs before I signed on with you lot."

Annette grinned. "Below the boards? Jo Dean, I'm shocked. Where would we find him, then?"

"Little Clams," Jo and Svetlana said in unison.

Annette's brow furrowed. "Where's that?"

"It's a brothel in the Unfathomed Enclave," Svetlana said, setting one of the spice tins on the map beside a crescent-shaped archipelago. "Dargon basically runs the whole enclave." She shook her head. "It's a bit out of the way, and then we'd have to deal with Dargon."

"And I'd rather not take the ship into the Enclave if we can help it," Jo said. "A lot of the islands were mountains once, and not all of them have good landing docks, so it's more like tie your ship to an outcropping and hope a geyser eruption doesn't destabilize the rock you picked."

"Not to mention his—" Svetlana shuddered. "What's he call it, citadel?"

Jo nodded, adding a shudder of her own.

"Okay, clearly I'm missing something, not having been born to a life of piracy like you two," Annette said.

Svetlana chuckled. "Neither of us was born to it, we've just spent more time in its clutches. Dargon's got what he likes to call his own marvel of modern engineering, though I suspect there's nothing short of magic that could accomplish what he did." She illustrated her next sentence with a fist atop her opposite flattened palm. "They sheared off the top of one of the islands, flipped it, and chucked it over a geyser. Nobody I know can really explain how they did it or how it works, but he's got a floating chunk of rock that looks like a platform city. Only it shifts a lot, so what's flat one minute might be sloped the next." Svetlana demonstrated this, too, with her hand, holding it out level with the table and then tilting it at an improbable angle.

"Right," Annette said. She took three of the tins from Svetlana and placed them at Crullfeld, Thorpes, and Langdale, then stood back to study the map. "I'm guessing Heliopolis is off the table?"

"It's our last resort, I think, especially since that address is in the part of town where there's a strong Air Fleet presence. I wouldn't wish that errand on any of our friends, either," Svetlana said.

"And if we don't want to go to this Unfathomed Enclave, is there another way to find Dargon's ships?" Annette asked.

"They make the same stops we often do. We can ask around wherever we wind up taking cargo to, and see if they've been spotted recently," Jo said.

"Worst case, we send a message from Rrusadon to Chickie and see if he can either get the information from his contacts or maybe Narci," Svetlana added, dropping the last tin at Rrusadon.

A clatter of tools in the corner drew the women's attention to Indigo and Deliah. The girl was staring at them, a strange expression on her face, and her lips moved slightly under the cover of one of her hands.

"What is it, Deliah?" Svetlana asked, narrowing her good eye at the girl.

Deliah shook her head slowly, then turned back toward Drassilis.

"What was that about?" Jo asked.

Svetlana turned back to the map. "No idea."

Indigo yelped, and the women turned back to him. Deliah leapt up from the floor and scurried out of the mess, while Indigo shielded his bright pink face from Drassilis's flailing arms.

"He's working!" Svetlana said, leaping up from her chair. "Annette, grab Indy. Jo, where'd we put the net?"

"On the bridge," Jo said, rising from her chair slowly, wide gaze fixed on Drassilis.

The automaton began to make noises, unintelligible, but as though his voice box were back up and running. His flailing continued, now accompanied by sparks.

Annette grabbed Indigo and pulled him away from Drassilis's lower half. The boy let her pull him away, though he remained bright pink, in contrast to his shockingly blue hair.

Svetlana looked at Indigo. "Where's the bicarbonate?"

"Engine room," Indigo choked out.

Turning to Jo, Svetlana gave her a quick nod. The pilot ran out of the mess in the direction of the engines.

"There's none up here?" Annette exclaimed.

Svetlana glanced at Annette and hurried into the kitchen, leaping over Drassilis's prone and flailing body. His voice still stuttered, but now it had settled mostly on saying "all" or something like it over and over.

Svetlana rummaged through the tins in the cupboard, not worrying about which ones fell to the kitchen floor around her. She seized on the tin of sodium bicarbonate and pulled off the lid, disappointed to find only a small amount remaining. Watching Drassilis's body carefully, she sprinkled a bit toward the areas where the most sparks were erupting. Drassilis's convulsions slowed.

"Oh, sweet Skyfather, did I break him again?" Svetlana asked.

"M-m-m-m-uth," Drassilis said. His hands found purchase on the mess floor, and he pulled himself into a semi-sitting position. "Mother."

Svetlana let out a deep, shuddering sigh. "Your mother's not here, Drassilis."

Drassilis's large eyes blinked shut, then reopened slowly. "Mother to us all. Mother is not here."

"You did it, Indy!" Jo exclaimed, returning to the doorway of the mess with the larger bucket of sodium bicarbonate that they kept in case of fires in the engine room. "He's back!"

"Mother is not back. Mother to us all is not back."

"Hi, Drassilis, good to see you too," Jo said. "No need for the bicarbonate, then?"

"Doesn't look like it," Svetlana said. "A little sprinkle did it."

"Sprinkle. Mother to us all." Drassilis said.

"Okay, that's going to get annoying really fast if that's all he can say," Jo said.

Athos poked his head into the mess. "Oh, hey, the creepy automaton is working! Is that why Deliah was running like a bat out of the abyss?"

Svetlana shrugged. "Could be. Cargo?"

"Nothing for the directions we want to go," he replied with a shrug. "Mostly stuff bound for Heliopolis or places to the east."

"Alright, well let's get this disaster area cleaned up," Svetlana said. "Indy, you want to come with me to find Deliah?"

The boy shook his head.

"What? Why not?" Svetlana asked.

"Deliah's gone."

# CHAPTER THIRTEEN

"Why is Deliah gone, Indy?" Svetlana asked. "What happened?"

The boy shrugged his slender shoulders. "She said she knew how to fix Drassilis, but if she did, she would have to go. So she—" He pressed his lips tightly together. "She did a thing, and then Drassilis was fixed, so she left."

"Did a thing?" Jo asked. "Like what, pushed a button?"

Indigo nodded. "Must have."

"You didn't see what she did," Athos said. "She distracted you, huh?"

Indigo blushed crimson, and he looked away from Athos. "She kissed me."

Svetlana chuckled. "That's one way to distract someone. Clever girl." She turned her attention to Drassilis, who had stopped squawking about "mother to us all." "You alright, Drassilis?"

"I am at roughly twenty percent of my capacity, and I do not believe I am capable of moving from this location. Where is Mother?"

"She's not here," Jo said. "Cap'n, I know you want information about the Bartram Cask, but we may have a different problem to deal with. Indy, did Deliah say where she had to go if she fixed Drassilis?"

Indigo shook his head, then frowned. "Not really. Not a real place, anyway."

"What sort of fake place was it, then?" Jo asked.

"She said she had to go see her mother. But she doesn't have a mother."

"Everyone has a mother," Annette said, with a glance at Drassilis. "Some folks end up with more than one. Did she say anything more than that she needed to see her mother?"

"She said it the way Drassilis says it. Mother to us all."

Svetlana froze, her spine rigid. "What?"

"Mother to us all," Indigo repeated.

"Mother to us all," Drassilis intoned.

"Lady de Whittvy," Svetlana said. "Mother to us all, at least on Bonebriar." She glanced around at the crew, not sure how much she wanted to say within Drassilis's earshot. "Let's take this conversation upstairs. Indy, you want to finish cleaning up down here, and keep Drassilis company for a bit?"

"Yes, Captain," Indigo said, picking up the tin of bicarbonate and shuffling around the mess.

Svetlana led the remaining crew members up to the bridge. "I don't think I'm ready to tell Drassilis that his mother is dead. So let's keep that between us, got it?"

Athos and Annette nodded immediately, and Jo joined in a moment later.

"Okay," Svetlana continued. "So Deliah went to find Lady de Whittvy? I don't even know when Deliah might have heard her called 'Mother to us all,' but there's no one else I know with that sobriquet."

"They were both on a ghost ship, for a bit, at least," Athos said.

Svetlana nodded. "True, though I really don't get the impression Lady de Whittvy went around introducing herself as 'hello, I'm a brilliant scientist and noblewoman who moonlights as a sneak thief, but everyone calls me Mother.' It's not her style."

"And that's not how she introduced herself to us," Annette added. "Though I suppose Drassilis did that part of the introduction. She at least never asked us to call her Mother. So if Deliah's decided that Lady de Whittvy is Mother to us all, then that's probably on Deliah."

"Okay, so let's say Deliah's gone to find Lady de Whittvy, somehow." Svetlana shook her head. "That implies she's alive, right? How does Deliah know that and we don't?"

"They were both on a ghost ship," Athos repeated, his voice low. "Now, go along with me for a second here. Lady de Whittvy and Deliah were on a ghost ship before. Lady de Whittvy was their prisoner, and then they picked up Deliah from Heliopolis."

"Yeah, did we ever ask Deliah why they blew out the back of a house and took her onboard?" Jo asked.

Svetlana shook her head. "With all the places that girl's been in her short life, I don't tend to ask many questions about how she's wound up there. Half the time, I think she's got wings or something."

"Unlikely," Athos said. "But I'm not done yet. We haven't gotten a straight answer out of Deliah as to why a ghost ship picked her up, but they did. Then, after Bonebriar, Deliah disappeared again. And when we found her, it was because a ghost ship dropped her off at Heatbourne. And she complained about that ghost ship not having the right ghosts?"

"Yeah," Svetlana said, brow furrowing. "Something about them not having any nice ghosts."

Athos splayed out his hands, palms up, on the navigation table that the crew stood around. "We may not know if Lady de Whittvy's alive or dead, to be honest, but if she were dead, what are the odds that she's somehow back on a ghost ship?"

Svetlana's jaw dropped. She tried to contradict him, but every explanation that came into her mind was something she could immediately shoot back down. His idea was sound. If Lady de Whittvy had died in her arms on Bonebriar, had become a ghost, why wouldn't she wind up back on a ghost ship, where she'd apparently made friends during her previous stay?

"You're saying she's become an actual ghost," Jo said, finally breaking the silence after Athos's revelation. "As though actual ghosts are actually real."

"Aetherwhere," Svetlana said, regaining her capacity for speech. "We've been there. We were on that ship. There are beings existing within that space, and I think calling them ghosts is fine."

Annette looked over the map on the navigation table. "Deliah knows where the Gyrfalcon staves are." She rifled through the papers around the map. "Did one of you grab the list that Elwisia gave us?"

Svetlana, Jo, and Athos all shook their heads.

"I doubt Indy had the presence of mind, after having just been kissed by a girl he likes, to grab it," Athos said.

"Then she has the list, too," Annette said. "She's got the list, she knows about Dargon, and she's probably taking that list and information to, well, assuming Athos is right, Lady de Whittvy and the ghosts."

"Then we need to get moving," Svetlana said. "We need to find the staves before anyone else does, if for no other reason than to keep them away from the Air Fleet. And the ghosts, it seems."

~

Svetlana sat on the bridge as Jo took off from Bluesummer, trying to recreate the list that Elwisia had given them. The map they had laid out on the mess table was now on the bridge, but it had only tins marking the cities, not the list of addresses within each city. "Jo, was it three buildings in Langdale and two in Thorpes, or the other way around?"

Jo frowned as though in concentration. "Where's Athos?"

"Below, I suspect. You need him for something?"

"I need someone on the spyglass."

Svetlana rose to approach the speaking tube that went below decks, but paused before she got there. "Would you need that spyglass to identify the ship that appears to be following us?"

Jo nodded. "Looks like maybe your girlfriend stuck around to see where we went next."

"Narci wasn't on an Air Fleet ship," Svetlana said. "And that one's navy and red." She took long strides to reach the speaking tube cover and kick it open. "Indy, we're going to need a bit of speed. Athos, aft cannon. Don't fire unless they fire on us. Annette, come topside." Svetlana left the tube open and stood next to Jo. "You want my help up here?"

"Speaking tube, maybe. Just in case they seem more inclined to chat than to shoot." Jo chuckled. "But I suspect the way of the Fleet right now is shoot first when it comes to Captain Tereshchenko."

Svetlana nodded, watching the Air Fleet ship as it approached on their port side. It was a much larger vessel than *The Silent Monsoon*, which meant it had bigger and more powerful engines. Outrunning it wasn't an option. Outmaneuvering it was possible, on a cloudy day, but the skies around Bluesummer were, predictably, clear and blue, in spite of the chilly temperatures on the ground. "Thoughts?" she asked Jo.

"If they want to knock us out of the sky, they'll have no problem doing so. That they haven't yet suggests to me that that's not their plan. So they either want to talk, or they want to capture us and then talk. Can you read the name yet?"

Svetlana squinted at the gold lettering on the starboard bow of the ship that pursued them. Just as she was preparing to shake her head, Annette slipped up behind her and said, "*Stoessel*. We know that one, right?"

"Know of it," Svetlana confirmed. "Captain Fisher. We haven't had the pleasure yet."

"Well, you said she's a lady captain, right?" Jo asked. "You could just seduce her."

Svetlana shook her head. "Yes, I'm sure that'll work just fine. She's here to ask me about some sort of Fleet business, and I just start wooing her right then and there."

"Athos would," Jo grumbled.

"Then let's get him up here," Svetlana said. "Honestly, Jo Dean, we're at a big disadvantage here, on a lot of levels. So any plans you have that don't involve me seducing an Air Fleet captain? I'm all ears."

"It might be too late for a plan," Annette said. "They're coming up alongside, and they've got boarding gear."

*The Silent Monsoon* jerked suddenly, and Jo yelped. "That wasn't me. They just bumped us."

Athos's voice came up from below. "They're blocking our gun ports."

"Get up here, bring your guns," Svetlana said, drawing her own pistols. "Annette?"

The doctor nodded, unholstering her gun. She glanced back at Jo.

"Left boot," Jo said.

Annette hurried around the steering column and crouched to get the gun from Jo's boot.

"Don't let them get on the bridge," Jo said as Svetlana and Annette headed onto the deck.

"We'll try," Svetlana said.

Across the narrow space between the ships, a dozen Air Fleet personnel stood at the ready to board *The Silent Monsoon*. Though Jo was steering their ship away from the *Stoessel*, the pilot on the Air Fleet ship was keeping perfectly aligned beside Svetlana's ship. Thus far, the gap remained wide enough that the Air Fleet wasn't going to board the *Monsoon* yet. But even the slightest slip on Jo's part would change that.

Without the speaking tube, communications between the two ships were limited. The wind rushing past both ships killed virtually any words that either crew tried to speak. But Svetlana still cupped her hands around her mouth and shouted, "What do you want with us?"

No response came from the Air Fleet ship.

Svetlana raised her pistols, first leveling them at one of the aeronauts, but then raising the one in her right hand to aim at one of the *Stoessel*'s balloons instead. She turned her head to check her aim, then grinned at the other crew.

They'd be young ensigns, most likely, assigned to the boarding party, who had probably heard of the Butcher of Barkovia, a nickname that had been inaccurately applied to Svetlana years previous. Even with that reputation, though, they wouldn't know what to make of the madwoman with one bad eye and two loaded pistols pointing one of them at a balloon on their ship. A direct hit on one of their balloons wouldn't founder the airship immediately, but it would make them a lot less likely to continue their pursuit.

The *Stoessel* jerked toward *The Silent Monsoon*, knocking against the hull of Svetlana's ship. As one, the Air Fleet crew surged forward, dropping their hooked ladders to span the small gap between the ships and scurrying across them. Four aeronauts made it across before Jo recovered and steered *The Silent Monsoon* away from the *Stoessel*, the hooked ladders tearing away chunks of the port bulkhead. Several of the ladders clattered away, though the *Stoessel*'s crew maintained their grip on a couple of them.

The troops that had made it onto *The Silent Monsoon* were three women and one man, all slender and smaller in stature. They each drew a pair of guns as they approached Svetlana and Annette.

Behind them, Athos crept up from below decks and jammed his pistol into the back of one of the women's heads. She let out a gasp that was inaudible where Svetlana stood, but her shock still registered on her face. One of the other women turned to look at her, while the man and the third woman continued to approach Svetlana and Annette slowly.

Svetlana fired the pistol she held aloft toward one of the *Stoessel*'s balloons. No squealing hiss of heated air escaping the balloon followed, and she cursed beneath her breath that her posturing had been for naught. But she brought the pistol forward now, pulling back the hammer again. "What do you want with us?" she asked again.

The woman at the front spoke up. "Captain Svetlana Tereshchenko, you are wanted for questioning regarding the attack on Air Fleet officers at Bonebriar. We're here to bring you in."

"Oh, that?" Svetlana said with a laugh. "Okay, I suppose that makes some sense, but how do you plan on bringing me in? You're on my ship now, and your ladders went down."

Without a word, the woman shifted her guns to point at Annette. "Slow your ship, or we will fire on Doctor Campbell."

Svetlana didn't give her the chance. She fired both of her pistols at the woman, striking her in both shoulders. The woman screamed and dropped her guns.

But at the same time, the male ensign dropped to the ground. Svetlana shifted her attention to him. He moved quickly across the deck and onto the bridge.

"Jo!" Svetlana shouted, unsure if the pilot would be able to hear her over the sound of the rushing wind.

"Svetlana," Annette said softly, pointing toward the women that Athos had been dealing with. While the woman with Athos's pistol pressed to her scalp had raised her hands in surrender, the other stood atop what remained of the portion of the bulkhead nearest her.

"What—" Svetlana started.

The man who had scurried onto the bridge shouted through the speaking tube. "Heliopolis! Langdale! Thorpes! Crullfeld! The Unfathomed Enclave!"

The woman atop the bulkhead nodded and leapt toward the *Stoessel*. As soon as her feet had landed on the other ship's deck, the *Stoessel*'s engines went silent, allowing *The Silent Monsoon* to surge ahead of the *Stoessel*.

Svetlana screamed, "Dammit!" She started to pull back the hammers on her pistols, but Annette steadied her with a hand on her arm.

"It's too late." Annette shook her head. "They got what they came for."

Svetlana's shoulders slumped, but she gave Athos a quick nod. He relieved the woman he had kept his pistol trained on of her weapons, held her hands together behind her back, and marched her toward where Svetlana and Annette stood. Jo stood over the man who had slipped onto the bridge, a wicked looking knife poised over his neck.

Annette glanced at the woman who lay bleeding on the deck from the two shoulder wounds. "I guess I'd best see to her, huh?"

"May as well." Svetlana stomped onto the bridge and grabbed the man by the shoulders. "You wait outside with your friend and Lieutenant Tucker." Shoving him roughly, she slammed the door to the bridge and looked at Jo.

"Well, I guess in this case, maybe it's a good thing Deliah has the list," Jo suggested, shrugging as she did.

"Small blessings," Svetlana grumbled. "Let's get rid of these interlopers and then get out of this airspace."

~

With the boarding aeronauts returned to Bluesummer to await their own transportation, *The Silent Monsoon* was headed back toward Rrusadon.

Athos shook his head as he ran his hands over the port bulkheads. "It's not significant enough damage that I think we need to stop for long enough for an overhaul. Though sooner or later, she's going to need one."

"I'm thinking we just string nets across the gaps for now," Svetlana said. "If anyone else boards us, they can deal with getting tangled up in rope."

"That'll do. Do we have a plan?"

"Crullfeld's only got one location, and I recall that one. It's a tavern. So that should be easy enough if we flash some silver, buy some drinks, ask about their purchase of wood from the Gyrfalcons five years ago, and hope the answer isn't 'firewood.'"

Athos winced. "Do you really think someone would buy wood just to burn it? In a place like Crullfeld? They've got peat fields for days, don't they?"

"I'm pretty hopeful that we won't have to worry about those staves having been burned. What I don't understand is how the staves got split between so many locations. There's what, thirty or forty staves that the Gyrfalcons sold, and they've wound up in about ten different locations?" She ticked off the list on her fingers. "The Gyrfalcon estate, the vineyard, Crullfeld, Heliopolis, five buildings between Langdale and Thorpes, and one or more of Dargon's ships."

"And there were at least a dozen staves at Bluesummer, between the table and the fence," Athos said. "You're right, it doesn't make much sense that people would buy single staves or even two or three at a time. There must have been some other wood the Gyrfalcons were selling. I just can't imagine it would have worked in any other way."

"If they took the thing apart for scrap, you'd think someone would have seen the markings on them, wouldn't you?" Svetlana asked.

Athos shrugged. "It depends how many staves had markings, I suppose. Just one or two, they might have thought it was just imperfections in the wood."

Svetlana nodded, rubbing her chin. "Let's go inside, I've got some calculations to do."

Svetlana and Athos stepped back onto the bridge, and Jo looked up from the controls. "How bad is it?"

"We're still aloft," Athos said with a chuckle. "It's nothing serious, for now at least."

Svetlana pulled a stool over to the large map. "Alright, Lady de Whittvy had fourteen staves, according to what was on the film. That came from three casks, so that's roughly five useful staves per cask, right?"

Jo and Athos nodded.

"But the Silver Cask had seven, and the Somerset had ten, which throws off the average considerably. We've gotten two from the Gyrfalcon Cask so far, so how many of these other locations are going to have information we need, and how many will come up empty?"

"And how many were in the Bartram Cask?" Athos asked.

"I suppose we haven't had much of a chance to find out if Drassilis knows that information," Jo said.

Svetlana snapped her fingers. "You're right. Alright, keep us en route to Rrusadon. I'll go talk to the automaton."

Making her way down to the mess, Svetlana heard Indigo and Drassilis talking.

"Where did she go?" Indigo asked.

"To find Mother," Drassilis said.

"Why?" Svetlana asked, stepping into the doorway.

Drassilis's head rotated toward the sound of her voice, and he blinked his over-large eyes. "Mother must have called to her."

Svetlana gnawed at the inside of her lip. As far as she knew, no one had told Drassilis of Lady de Whittvy's fate. And though it seemed that the automaton should eventually be told, she was hesitant to tell him right now. She wasn't sure how he might react to learning that his "mother" was dead, but possibly also now a ghost. Instead, she asked what she had come down here for. "Drassilis, did your mother ever talk about the Bartram Cask?"

"Of course, Captain Tereshchenko. She hoped to acquire the information contained within."

Svetlana frowned. "She hadn't acquired that information already?"

"Ah, I see," Drassilis replied. "Yes, she had recently acquired the cask, but had not yet extracted the information. My understanding is that she hoped to do so on the evening she was taken by the ghosts."

"So then where was she keeping the cask?"

Drassilis blinked twice. "Why, in the cellar."

Svetlana slapped her forehead and groaned. "We were there, and the cask was there, and no one thought to tell us that information?"

"It must not have been pressing to Mother at the time," he replied.

"Of course," Svetlana said, shaking her head. "Well, I suppose you and your mother were the only ones with that information?"

"I believe that to be the case."

Svetlana frowned. If Athos's theory was right, the ghosts could have that information too. She wondered whether ghosts could go through the walls of the cask and retrieve the data from the staves that way. It seemed within the realm of their otherworldly capabilities, at least. Of course, that assumed that the Air Fleet had not returned to Bonebriar to have someone sift through the ruins. If they had, they might have the cask itself.

"Captain Tereshchenko, I have asked Indigo, but he does not know the answer. When might I see Mother?"

Svetlana swallowed hard. "Drassilis, your mother ... she had an accident."

"Oh." His voice seemed even more flat than his strange automaton voice. "I see. Then she will not rejoin us?"

"I'm afraid not, Drassilis. I'm sorry."

The automaton bowed his head for a moment, then said, "Mother always said that the frailty of her human form would be her downfall. She had hoped to someday construct a suit similar to my body that could be used to protect and preserve her for all time. It is a shame that her plan did not come to fruition in a timely fashion."

Svetlana forced a smile. "That it is, Drassilis. I would be right beside you in welcoming her back if she had managed to preserve herself in such a way."

Drassilis nodded unsteadily, but said nothing more.

After letting the silence hang between them for a few minutes, Svetlana cleared her throat. "So, what happens next for you, Drassilis?" she asked.

"I am not sure yet, Captain Tereshchenko."

"You're welcome to come with us, if you'd like to stay on our ship. Or we can drop you off somewhere else if you like."

"Thank you for the offer, Captain Tereshchenko. I must ... I will let you know my answer once I have made a decision."

"That's fine, Drassilis. I understand." Svetlana walked over and patted the automaton on his shoulder. The metal rang hollowly beneath her hand. She wasn't entirely sure how having an automaton on her crew might work out in the long run, but it was the least she could do for the grieving creature. As he looked up at her with his unblinking eyes, she gave him a stiff smile. "Alright, then. Good talk."

# CHAPTER FOURTEEN

Crullfeld reeked of peat and dampness that permeated the soil and the buildings, even more than Merrowbarrow had. Even the tavern with fires burning in two hearths and crowded with people couldn't completely obliterate the odor. Of course, the fuel for the fires was likely peat rather than wood, and all these people also smelled of Crullfeld's primary export. Svetlana wasn't sure if Athos really had gotten the worst of the deal, as he was out in the fresher air, checking the exterior of the tavern, while she and Jo ventured inside.

"You promise we'll be in and out of here fast, right?" Jo asked, winding a scarf across her lower face as she spoke.

"That's the plan," Svetlana said, scanning the tavern. "We'll find someone who knows something about the place, find the staves, and then we can leave."

Jo glanced around. "I see a couple of dark spots here and there on the walls. I'll check on those."

"Don't forget to check the tables, too," Svetlana reminded her. "Tops and bottoms."

"Why Cap'n, are you suggesting I flip some tables?" Jo smirked.

Svetlana shook her head and gave Jo a wry grin. "I don't recommend it, not unless that's the only option. Getting out of here without causing a fuss shouldn't be that hard, should it now?"

"You take all the fun out of it," Jo grumbled. "Alright, I'll keep a low profile. Just hurry. I don't want to be on this Skyfather-forsaken rock any longer than I have to be."

Svetlana approached the bar, looking over the three young men who worked there. They looked similar enough to be brothers, with their nearly jet-black hair, pale skin, and various smatterings of freckles, but even the eldest of them barely looked like he might have been working the bar five years previous. Still, she decided to aim for flattery. "You own this place?" she asked the seemingly eldest boy.

"Nah, me ma does," he said, his thickly accented voice close to laughter.

"Where's she, then?"

"Left us in charge while she's out," he replied. "What're ya drinking?"

"Ale," Svetlana said, reaching for her purse. "Two, please." She pulled a silver coin out and placed it on the counter, keeping it pinned with a single finger. "How well do you know this tavern?"

"Like the back'a me own hand. I's born right o'er there." He pointed toward the table that Jo was examining closely.

Svetlana scrutinized him. The faintest scruff of a mustache decorated his upper lip. She still couldn't tell his age, but he looked only a year or two older than Indigo. "Do you know if there was a new place built around here five years ago?"

"The cellar," he said. "After Pa's gone, Ma had it built." He shook his head. "Piece'a work, that. Dug in from the side, shored it all up, and then filled back in around it. Shame it's all for naught, though."

"How's that, then?" Svetlana asked, accepting the two mugs of ale.

"Ma wanted it for storage, but the only thing it's storing now is water. And not the kind you'll want to drink, neither."

"Sorry, I don't think I follow," Svetlana said, a frown creasing her brow.

"Cellar filled up with water from the ground," the boy replied with a shrug. "Ain't good for nothing except boiling for the wash."

"It's flooded," Svetlana said, her voice flat as she finally made sense of what he was saying. "Is there a way to get down there?"

"Fancying a swim?" he asked, his gaze flickering toward a nearby corner for an instant. "Shouldn't go before you've had your ale, and I wouldn't recommend it after, neither. All sorts of nasty beasties down there, too."

Svetlana gave him a quick nod. "Understood."

Jo took one of the ales from Svetlana before the captain even had a chance to offer it. As she pulled her scarf off her face, she said, "Nothing on the inside of the walls, and nothing on the tables I've seen so far. Three more to check."